W9-CMS-943

WITHDRAWN

IN THE LABYRINTH

A NOVEL BY ALAIN ROBBE-GRILLET

TRANSLATED BY RICHARD HOWARD

GROVE PRESS, INC. / NEW YORK

Copyright © 1960 by Grove Press, Inc.

Originally published in 1959 by Les Éditions de Minuit,
Paris, France, as *Dans le Labyrinthe*

Library of Congress Catalog Card Number: 60-11099

Typography by Diane Dorr-Dorynek

First Printing

Distributed in Canada by
McClelland & Stewart Ltd., 25 Hollinger Road,
Toronto 16

MANUFACTURED IN THE UNITED STATES OF AMERICA

This narrative is not a true account, but fiction. It describes a reality not necessarily the same as the one the reader has experienced: for example, in the French army, infantrymen do not wear their serial numbers on their coat collars. Similarly, the recent history of Western Europe has not recorded an important battle at Reichenfels or in the vicinity. Yet the reality in question is a strictly material one; that is, it is subject to no allegorical interpretation. The reader is therefore requested to see in it only the objects, actions, words, and events which are described, without attempting to give them either more or less meaning than in his own life, or his own death.

A. R.-G.

I am alone here now, under cover. Outside it is raining, outside you walk through the rain with your head down, shielding your eyes with one hand while you stare ahead nevertheless, a few yards ahead, at a few yards of wet asphalt; outside it is cold, the wind blows between the bare black branches; the wind blows through the leaves, rocking whole boughs, rocking them, rocking, their shadows swaying across the white roughcast walls. Outside the sun is shining, there is no tree, no bush to cast a shadow, and you walk under the sun shielding your eyes with one hand while you stare ahead, only a few yards in front of you, at a few yards of dusty asphalt where the wind makes patterns of parallel lines, forks, and spirals.

The sun does not get in here, nor the wind,

nor the rain, nor the dust. The fine dust which dulls the gloss of the horizontal surfaces, the varnished wood of the table, the waxed floor, the marble shelf over the fireplace, the marble top of the chest, the cracked marble on top of the chest, the only dust comes from the room itself: from the cracks in the floor maybe, or else from the bed, or from the curtains or from the ashes in the fireplace.

On the polished wood of the table, the dust has marked the places occupied for a while—for a few hours, several days, minutes, weeks—by small objects subsequently removed whose outlines are still distinct for some time, a circle, a square, a rectangle, other less simple shapes, some partly overlapping, already blurred or half obliterated as though by a rag.

When the outline is distinct enough to permit the shape to be identified with certainty, it is easy to find the original object again, not far away. For example, the circular shape has obviously been left by a glass ashtray which is lying beside it. Similarly, a little farther away, the square occupying the table's left rear corner corresponds to the base of the brass lamp that now stands in the right corner: a square pedestal about one inch high capped by a disk of the same height supporting a fluted column at its center.

The lampshade casts a circle of light on the

ceiling, but this circle is not complete: it is in-
tersected by the wall behind the table. This wall,
instead of being papered like the other three, is
concealed from floor to ceiling and for the greater
part of its width by thick red curtains made of
a heavy velvety material.

Outside it is snowing. Across the dark asphalt
of the sidewalk the wind is driving the fine dry
crystals which after each gust form white parallel
lines, forks, spirals that are immediately broken
up, seized by the eddies driven along the ground,
then immobilized again, recomposing new spirals,
scrolls, forked undulations, shifting arabesques
immediately broken up. You walk with your head
a little farther down, pressing the hand shielding
your eyes closer, leaving only a few inches of
ground visible in front of your feet, a few grayish
inches where your feet appear one after the other
and vanish behind you, one after the other, alternately.

But the staccato sound of hobnail boots on the
asphalt, coming steadily closer down the straight
street, sounding louder and louder in the calm
of the frostbound night, the sound of boots cannot come in here, any more than other sounds
from outside. The street is too long, the curtains
too thick, the house too high. No noise, even muffled, ever penetrates the walls of the room, no
vibration, no breath of air, and in the silence tiny

particles descend slowly, scarcely visible in the
lamplight, descend gently, vertically, always at
the same speed, and the fine gray dust lies in
a uniform layer on the floor, on the bedspread,
on the furniture.

On the waxed floor, the felt slippers have
made gleaming paths from the bed to the chest,
from the chest to the fireplace, from the fireplace
to the table. And on the table, the shifting of objects has also disturbed the continuity of the film
of dust; the latter, more or less thick according
to the length of time the surfaces have been exposed, is even occasionally interrupted altogether: as distinct as though drawn with a draft-
ing-pen, a square of varnished wood thus occupies the left rear corner, not precisely at the
corner of the table but parallel to its edges, set
back about four inches. The square itself is about
six inches on each side, and in it the reddish-
brown wood gleams, virtually without any deposit.

To the right, a simple shape that is vaguer,
already covered by several days' dust, can nevertheless still be recognized; from a certain angle
it is even distinct enough so that its outlines can
be followed without too much uncertainty. It
is a kind of cross: an elongated main section
about the size of a table knife but wider, pointed
at one end and broadening slightly at the other,

cut perpendicularly by a much shorter cross-piece; this latter is composed of two flaring appendages symmetrically arranged on each side of the axis at the base of its broadening portion—that is, about a third of the way from the wider end. It resembles a flower, the terminal widening representing a long closed corolla at the end of the stem with two small lateral leaves beneath. Or else it might be an approximately human statuette: an oval head, two very short arms, and the body terminating in a point toward the bottom. It might also be a dagger, with its handle separated by a guard from the wide, rounded, double-edged blade.

Still farther to the right, in the direction indicated by the tip of the flower, or by the point of the dagger, a slightly dusty circle is tangent to a second circle the same size, the latter not reduced to its mere outline on the table: the glass ashtray. Then come uncertain, overlapping shapes probably left by various papers whose successive changes of position have blurred their outlines, which in some places are quite distinct, in others obscured by dust, and in still others more than half obliterated, as though by a rag.

Beyond stands the lamp, in the right corner of the table: a square base six inches on each side, a disk tangent with its sides, of the same diameter, a fluted column supporting a dark, slightly conical lampshade. A fly is moving slowly and steadily around the upper rim of the shade. It casts a distorted shadow on the ceiling in which no element of the original insect can be recognized: neither wings nor body nor feet; the creature has been transformed into a simple threadlike outline, not closed, a broken regular line resembling a hexagon with one side missing: the image of the incandescent filament of the electric bulb. This tiny open polygon lies tangent at one of its corners to the inner rim of the great circle of light cast by the lamp. It changes position slowly but steadily along the circumference. When it reaches the vertical wall it disappears into the folds of the heavy red curtain.

Outside it is snowing. Outside it has been snowing, it was snowing, outside it is snowing. The thick flakes descend gently in a steady, uninterrupted, vertical fall—for there is not a breath of air—in front of the high gray walls whose arrangement, the alignment of the roofs, the location of the doors and windows, cannot be distinguished clearly because of the snow. There must be identical rows of regular windows on each floor from one end of the straight street to the other.

A perpendicular crossroad reveals a second street just like the first: the same absence of traffic, the same high gray walls, the same blind windows, the same deserted sidewalks. At the corner of the sidewalk, a street light is on, although it is broad daylight. But it is a dull day which makes everything colorless and flat. Instead of the striking vistas these rows of houses should produce, there is only a crisscrossing of meaningless lines, the falling snow depriving the scene of all relief, as if this blurred view were merely badly painted on a bare wall.

Where the wall and ceiling meet, the fly's shadow, the enlarged image of the filament of the electric bulb, reappears and continues its circuit around the rim of the white circle cast by the lamp. Its speed is always the same: slow and steady. In the dark area to the left a dot of light appears, corresponding to a small, round hole in the dark parchment of the lampshade; it is not actually a dot, but a thin broken line, a regular hexagon with one side missing: another enlarged image, this one stationary, of the same luminous source, the same incandescent thread.

It is the same filament again, that of a similar or slightly larger lamp, which glows so uselessly at the crossroads, enclosed in its glass cage on top of a cast-iron pedestal, a gas light with old-fashioned ornaments that has been converted into an electric street light.

Around the conical base of the cast-iron pedestal that widens toward the bottom and is ringed by several more or less prominent moldings, are embossed the slender stems of a stylized spray of ivy: curling tendrils; pointed, five-lobed, palmate leaves, their five veins very prominent where the scaling black paint reveals the rusted metal. Slightly higher a hip, an arm, a shoulder are leaning against the shaft of the lamppost. The man is wearing a faded military overcoat of no particular color, perhaps once green or khaki. His face is grayish; his features are drawn and give the impression of extreme fatigue, but perhaps a beard more than a day old is largely responsible for this impression. Prolonged waiting, prolonged immobility in the cold may also have drained the color from his cheeks, forehead, and lips.

The eyelids are gray, like the rest of the face; they are lowered. The head is bowed. The eyes are looking at the ground, that is, at the edge of the snow-covered sidewalk in front of the base of the street light and the two heavy marching boots with rounded toes whose coarse leather shows scratches and other signs of wear and tear, more or less covered by the black polish. The layer of snow is not thick enough to yield visibly underfoot, so that the soles of the boots are resting—or virtually resting—on the level of the white snow extending around them. At the edge of the sidewalk, this surface is completely unmarked, not shining but smooth, even, delicately stippled with its original granulation. A little snow has accumulated on the upper edge of the last projecting ring that encircles the widening base of the lamppost, forming a white circle above the black circle by which the latter rests on the ground. Higher up, some flakes have also stuck to other asperities of the cone, accenting the successive rings and the upper edges of the ivy leaves with a white line, as well as all the fragments of stems and veins that are horizontal or only slightly inclined.

But the bottom of the overcoat has swept away several of these tiny agglomerations, just as the boots, changing position several times, have trampled the snow in their immediate vicinity, leaving in places yellower areas, hardened, half-raised pieces and the deep marks of hobnails arranged in alternate rows. In front of the chest, the felt slippers have cleared a large gleaming area in the dust, and another one in front of the table at the place that must be occupied by a desk chair or an armchair, a stool or some kind of seat. A narrow path of gleaming floor has been made from one to the other; a second path goes from the table to the bed. Parallel to the house-fronts, a little closer to the walls than to the gutter, a yellowish-gray straight path also indicates the snow-covered sidewalk. Produced by the footsteps of people now gone, the path passes between the lighted street light and the door of the last apartment house, then turns at right angles and disappears in the perpendicular cross street, still following the line of the housefronts about a third of the way across the sidewalk, from one end of its length to the other.

Another path then leads from the bed to the chest. From here, the narrow strip of gleaming floor which leads from the chest to the table, joining the two large areas cleared of dust, swerves slightly in order to pass closer to the fireplace whose grate contains a heap of ashes, without andirons. The black marble of the mantlepiece, like everything else, is covered with gray dust. But the layer is not so thick as on the table or on the floor, and it is uniform on the entire surface of the shelf; now no object encumbers the shelf, and only one has left its outlines, clear and black, in the exact center of the rectangle. This is the same four-branched cross: one branch elongated and pointed, one shorter and oval, the continuation of the first, and two small flaring appendages set perpendicularly on each side.

A similar design also embellishes the wallpaper. The wallpaper is pale gray with slightly darker vertical stripes; between the dark stripes, in the middle of each lighter stripe, runs a line of small dark-gray identical designs: a rosette, some kind of clove, or a tiny torch whose handle consists of what was just now the blade of a dagger, the dagger handle now representing the flame, and the two lateral flaring appendages which were the dagger's guard now representing the little cup which keeps the burning substance from running down the handle.

But it might be a kind of electric torch instead, for the tip of what is supposed to produce the light is clearly rounded like an oblong bulb instead of being pointed like a flame. The design, reproduced thousands of times up and down the walls all around the room, is a simple silhouette about the size of a large insect, of a uniform color so that it is difficult to make it out: it reveals no greater relief than the incandescent filament which must be inside the bulb. Besides, the bulb is hidden by the lampshade. Only the image of the filament is visible on the ceiling: a small, open hexagon appearing as a luminous line against the dim background, and farther to the right an identical small hexagon, but in motion, silhouetted against the circle of light cast by the lamp, advancing slowly, steadily, along the inner rim until it reaches the vertical wall and disappears.

The soldier is carrying a package under his left arm. His right arm, from shoulder to elbow, is leaning against the lamppost. His head is turned toward the street, showing his growth of beard and the serial number on the collar of his overcoat, five or six black figures in a red diamond. Behind him the double door of the corner apartment house is not completely closed—not ajar either, but one leaf simply pushed against the fixed one, which is narrower, leaving perhaps an inch or two of space between them, a vertical stripe of darkness. To the right is the row of ground floor windows interrupted only by the doors of the buildings, identical windows and identical doors, the latter similar to the windows in shape and size. There is not a single shop in sight from one end of the street to the other.

To the left of the door that is not closed tight, there are only two windows, then the corner of the building, then, at right angles, another row of identical windows and doors which look like the reflection of the first, as if a mirror had been set there, making an obtuse angle (a right angle increased by half a right angle) with the plane of the housefronts; and the same series is repeated: two windows, a door, four windows, a door, etc. . . . The first door is ajar on a dark hallway, leaving between its two unequal leaves a dark interval wide enough for a man, or at least a child, to slip through.

In front of the door, at the edge of the side-

walk, a street light is on, although it is still daylight. But the dim and diffuse light of this
snowy landscape makes the light from the electric bulb apparent at first glance: somewhat
brighter, a little yellower, a little more localized.
Against the base of the street light a bareheaded
soldier is leaning, his head lowered, his hands
hidden in his overcoat pockets. Under his right
arm is a package wrapped in brown paper that
looks something like a shoe box, with a white
string doubtless tied in a cross; but only that
part of this string around the length of the box
is visible, the other part, if it exists, being hidden by the overcoat sleeve. On this sleeve at
elbow level are several dark stains that may be
the remains of fresh mud, or paint, or grease.

The box wrapped in brown paper is now on
the chest. It no longer has its white string, and
the wrapping paper, carefully folded back along
the shorter side of the parallelepiped, gapes a
little in a sharp fold narrowing toward the bottom. At this point the marble top of the chest
shows a long, almost straight crack passing diagonally under the corner of the box and reaching
the wall toward the middle of the chest. Just
over it is hung the picture.

The picture framed in varnished wood, the
striped wallpaper, the fireplace with its heap of
ashes, the table with its lamp and its glass ash-

tray, the heavy red curtains, the large day bed covered with the same red velvety material, and finally the chest with its three drawers and its cracked marble top, the brown package on top of it, and above that the picture, and the vertical lines of little gray insects rising to the ceiling.

Outside, the sky remains the same dull white. It is still daylight. The street is empty: there is no traffic, and there are no pedestrians on the sidewalks. It has been snowing; and the snow has not yet melted. It forms a rather thin layer —an inch or so—which is quite regular, however, and covers all the horizontal surfaces with the same dull, neutral whitish color. The only interruptions visible are the straight paths parallel to the housefronts and the gutters (made even more distinct by their vertical curbs which have remained black) separating the sidewalks into two unequal strips for their entire length. At the crossroads, at the base of the street light, a small circle of trampled snow has the same yellowish color as the narrow paths that run alongside the buildings. The doors are closed. The windows show no figure either pressed against the panes or even looming farther back in the rooms. The flatness of this entire setting, moreover, suggests that there is nothing behind these panes, behind these doors, behind these housefronts. And the entire scene remains empty: without a man, a woman, or even a child.

The picture, in its varnished wood frame, represents a tavern scene. It is a nineteenth-century etching, or a good reproduction of one. A large number of people fill the room, a crowd of drinkers sitting or standing, and, on the far left, the bartender standing on a slightly raised platform behind his bar.

The bartender is a fat, bald man wearing an apron. He leans forward, both hands resting on the edge of the bar, over several half-full glasses that have been set there, his massive shoulders turned toward a small group of middle-class citizens in frock coats who appear to be engaged in an animated discussion; standing in various attitudes, many are making expansive gestures that sometimes involve the whole body, and are doubtless quite expressive.

To their right, that is, in the center of the scene, several groups of drinkers are sitting at tables that are irregularly arranged—or rather, crammed—in a space too small to hold them all comfortably. These men are also making extravagant gestures and their faces are violently contorted, but their movements, like their expressions, are frozen by the drawing, suspended, stopped short, which also makes their meaning uncertain; particularly since the words being shouted on all sides seem to have been absorbed by a thick layer of glass. Some of them, carried away by their excitement, have half risen from their chairs or their benches and are pointing over the heads of the others toward a more distant interlocutor. Everywhere hands rise, mouths open, heads turn; fists are clenched, pounded on tables, or brandished in mid-air.

At the far right a group of men, almost all workers judging from their clothes, like those sitting at the tables, have their backs to the latter and are crowding around some poster or picture tacked on the wall. A little in front of them, between their backs and the first row of drinkers facing in the other direction, a boy is sitting on the floor among all these legs with their shapeless trousers, all these clumsy boots stamping about and trying to move toward his left; on the other side he is partially protected by the bench. The child is shown facing straight ahead. He is sitting with his legs folded under him, his arms clasped around a large box something like a shoe box. No one is paying any attention to him. Perhaps he was knocked down in the confusion. As a matter of fact, in the foreground, not far from where he is sitting, a chair has been overturned and is still lying on the floor.

Somewhat apart, as though separated from the crowd surrounding them by an unoccupied zone—narrow, of course, but nevertheless wide enough for their isolation to be noticeable, in any case wide enough to call attention to them though they are in the background—three soldiers are sitting around a smaller table, the second from the rear on the right, their motionlessness and rigidity in marked contrast to the civilians who fill the room. The soldiers are looking straight ahead, their hands resting on the checkered oilcloth; there are no glasses in front of them. They are the only men whose heads are not bare, for they are wearing low-peaked fatigue caps. Behind them, at the extreme rear, the last seated drinkers are mingled with others who are standing, forming a confused mass; besides, the drawing here is vaguer too. Under the print, in the white margin, someone has written a title: "The Defeat of Reichenfels."

On closer examination, the isolation of the three soldiers seems to result less from the narrow space between them and the crowd than from the direction of the glances around them. All the figures in the background look as if they are passing—or trying to pass, for the space is cramped—behind the soldiers to reach the left side of the picture, where there is probably a door (though this hypothetical exit cannot be seen in the picture because of a row of coat racks covered with hats and coats); every head is looking straight ahead (that is, toward the coat racks), except for one here and there who turns to speak to someone who has remained in the rear. Everyone in the crowd gathered on the right is looking toward the right wall. The drinkers at the tables are represented in natural poses, turning toward the center of each group or else toward one neighbor or another. As for the middle-class citizens in front of the bar, they too are completely absorbed in their own conversation, and the bartender leans toward them without paying any attention to the rest of his customers. Among the various groups circulate a number of persons not yet settled, but obviously about to adopt one of several probable attitudes: either walking over to examine the bulletin board, sitting down at one of the tables, or else going out behind the coat racks; a moment's scrutiny is enough to reveal that each man has already determined what he is going to do next; here, as among the groups, no face, no movement betrays hesitation, perplexity, inner vacillation, or contradiction. The three soldiers, on the contrary, seem forsaken. They are not talking to each other; they are not looking at anything in particular: neither glasses, nor bulletins, nor their neighbors. They have nothing to do. No one looks at them and they themselves have nothing to look at. The position of their faces—one full face, the other in profile, the last in a three-quarters view—indicates no common subject of attention. Besides, the first man—the only one whose features are completely visible—betrays no expression whatever, merely a fixed, vacant stare.

The contrast between the three soldiers and the crowd is further accentuated by a precision of line, a clarity in rendering, much more evident in their case than in that of other individuals the same distance from the viewer. The artist has shown them with as much concern for detail and almost as much sharpness of outline as if they were sitting in the foreground. But the composition is so involved that this is not apparent at first glance. Particularly the soldier shown full face has been portrayed with a wealth of detail that seems quite out of proportion to the indifference it expresses. No specific thought can be discerned. It is merely a tired face, rather thin, and narrowed still further by several days' growth of beard. This thinness, these shadows that accentuate the features without, on the other hand, indicating the slightest individual characteristic, nevertheless emphasize the brilliance of the wide-open eyes.

The military overcoat is buttoned up to the neck, where the regimental number is embroidered on a diamond-shaped tab of material. The cap is set straight on the head, covering the hair, which is cut extremely short, judging from its appearance at the temples. The man is sitting stiffly, his hands lying flat on the table which is covered with a red-and-white checked oilcloth.

He has finished his drink some time ago. He does not look as if he were thinking of leaving. Yet, around him, the café has emptied. The light is dim now, the bartender having turned out most of the lamps before leaving the room himself.

The soldier, his eyes wide open, continues to stare into the half-darkness a few yards in front of him, where the child is standing, also motionless and stiff, his arms at his sides. But it is as if the soldier did not see the child—or anything else. He looks as if he has fallen asleep from exhaustion, sitting close to the table, his eyes wide open.

It is the child who speaks first. He says: "Are you asleep?" He has spoken almost in a whisper, as if he were afraid to awaken the sleeper. The latter has not stirred. After a few seconds the child repeats his question a trifle louder: "Are you asleep?" and he adds, in the same expressionless, slightly singsong tone of voice: "You can't sleep here, you know."

The soldier has not stirred. The child might suppose he is alone in the room, merely pretending to have a conversation with someone who does not exist, or else with a doll, a toy unable to answer. Under these conditions there was certainly no need to speak louder; the voice was actually that of a child telling himself a story.

But the voice has stopped, as if unable to struggle further against the silence which has prevailed again. The child, too, may have fallen asleep.

"No . . . Yes . . . I know," the soldier says.

Neither one has moved. The child is still standing in the half-darkness, his arms at his sides. He has not even seen the man's lips moving as he sits at the table under the one light bulb that is still on in the room; his head has not moved at all, his eyes have not even blinked, and his mouth is still closed.

"Your father . . ." the soldier begins. Then he stops. But this time the lips have stirred a little.

"He's not my father," the child says.

And he turns his head toward the door with its black rectangle of window glass in the upper half.

Outside it is snowing. The fine flakes have begun falling thickly again on the already white road. The wind has risen and is blowing them horizontally, so that the soldier has to keep his head down, a little farther down, as he walks, pressing the hand shielding his eyes still closer against his forehead, leaving visible only a few square inches of thin, crunching snow that is already trampled hard. Reaching a crossroad, the soldier hesitates and looks around for the plaques that should indicate the name of that cross street. But it is useless, for there are no blue enamel plaques here, or else they are set too high and the night is too dark; besides, the fine, close flakes quickly blind him when he tries to look up. Then too, a street name would hardly furnish him much in the way of helpful information: he does not know this city anyway.

He hesitates for another moment, looks ahead again, then back at the road he has just taken, with its rows of street lights whose circles of light, closer and closer together and increasingly dim, soon disappear in the darkness. Then he turns right, into the cross street which is also deserted, lined with the same kind of apartment houses and the same row of street lights, set fairly far apart but at regular intervals, their dim circles of light revealing as he passes the oblique fall of the snow.

The white flakes, falling thick and fast, suddenly change direction; vertical for a few seconds, they suddenly become almost horizontal. Then they stop suddenly and, with a sudden gust of wind, begin to blow at virtually the same angle in the opposite direction, which they abandon after two or three seconds just as abruptly as before, to return to their original orientation, making new, almost horizontal parallel lines that cross the circle of light from left to right toward the unlighted windows.

In the window recesses the snow has formed an uneven layer, very shallow on the sill but deeper toward the back, making an already considerable drift that fills the right corner and reaches as high as the pane. All the ground floor windows, one after the other, show exactly the same amount of snow which has drifted toward the right in the same way.

At the next crossroad, under the corner street light, a child is standing. He is partially hidden by the cast-iron shaft whose broader base conceals the lower part of his body altogether. He is watching the soldier approach. He does not seem bothered by the storm, or by the snow that whitens some of his black cape and his beret. He is a boy of about ten, his expression serious and alert. He turns his head as the soldier approaches him, watching him as he reaches the lamppost, then passes it. Since the soldier is not walking fast, the child has time to examine him carefully from head to foot: the unshaven cheeks, the apparent fatigue, the dirty ragged overcoat, the sleeves without chevrons, the wet package under his left arm, both hands thrust deep in his pockets, the hurriedly wrapped, irregular leggings, the wide gash down the back of the right boot, at least four inches long and so deep it looks as if it pierces the leather; yet the boot is not split and the damaged area has merely been smeared with black polish, which now gives it the same dark-gray color as the adjoining surfaces that are still intact.

The man has stopped. Without moving the rest of his body, he has turned his head around toward the child looking at him, already three steps away, already crisscrossed by many white lines.

A moment later, the soldier slowly pivots and takes a step toward the street light. The boy steps back, against the cast-iron shaft; at the same time he pulls the bottom of his cape around his legs, holding it from the inside without showing his hands. The man has stopped. Now that the gusts of snow are no longer striking him directly in the face, he can raise his head without too much trouble.

"Don't be afraid," he says.

He takes a step toward the child and repeats a little louder: "Don't be afraid."

The child does not answer. Without seeming to feel the thickly falling flakes that make him squint slightly, he continues to stare at the soldier directly in front of him. The latter begins:

"Do you know where . . ."

But he goes no further. The question he was going to ask is not the right one. A gust of wind blows the snow into his face again. He takes his right hand out of his overcoat pocket and shields his eyes with it. He has no glove, his fingers are red and dirty. When the gust is over he puts his hand back in his pocket.

"Where does this road go?"

The boy still says nothing. His eyes have left the soldier to look toward the end of the street in the direction the man has nodded toward; he sees only the succession of street lights, closer and closer together, dimmer and dimmer, which vanish into the darkness.

"What's the matter, are you afraid I'll eat you?"

"No," the child says. "I'm not afraid."

"Well then, tell me where this road goes."

"I don't know," the child says.

And he looks again at this badly dressed, unshaven soldier who does not even know where he is going. Then, without warning, he makes a sudden turn, skillfully avoids the base of the lamppost, and begins to run as fast as he can along the row of apartment houses, in the opposite direction from the way the soldier came. In a few seconds, he has disappeared.

At the next street light, he appears again for several seconds; he is still running just as fast; his cape billows out behind him. He reappears at each lamppost, once, twice, then no more.

The soldier turns back and continues on his way. Again the snow strikes him directly in the face.

He puts the package under his right arm to try to shield his face with his left hand, for the wind is blowing more continuously from this side. But he soon gives this up and puts his hand, numb with cold, back in his overcoat pocket. Now he merely turns his head away to get less snow in his eyes, tilting it toward the unlighted windows where the white drift continues to accumulate in the right-hand corner of the recess.

Yet it is this same boy with the serious expression who led him to the café run by the man who is not his father. And there was a similar scene under the same kind of lamppost, at an identical crossroads. Perhaps it was snowing a little less heavily. The flakes were thicker, heavier, slower. But the boy answered with just as much reticence, holding his black cape tight around his knees. He had the same alert expression and seemed to be just as untroubled by the snow. He hesitated just as long at each question before giving an answer which furnished his interlocutor no information. Where did the street go? A long silent stare toward the presumed end of the street, then the calm voice:

"To the boulevard."

"And this one?"

The boy slowly turns his eyes in the direction the man has just nodded toward. His features reveal no difficulty remembering, no uncertainty, when he repeats in the same expressionless tone:

"To the boulevard."

"The same one?"

Again there is silence, and the snow falling, slower and heavier.

"Yes," the boy says. Then, after a pause: "No," and finally, with a sudden violence: "It's the boulevard!"

"And is it far?" the soldier asks again.

The child is still looking at the series of street lights, closer and closer together, dimmer and dimmer, which here too vanish into the darkness.

"Yes," he says, his voice calm again and sounding as if it came from far away.

The soldier waits another minute to make

sure there will not be another "no." But the boy is already running along the row of apartment houses, down the trampled snow path the soldier followed in the opposite direction a few minutes earlier. When the running boy crosses a circle of light, his black cape billowing out behind him can be seen for a few seconds, once, twice, three times, smaller and vaguer at each reappearance, until there is nothing but a confused whirl of snow.

Yet it is certainly the same boy who walks ahead of the soldier when the latter comes to the café. Before crossing the threshold, the child shakes his black cape and takes off his beret, which he knocks twice against the door jamb in order to brush off the bits of ice which have formed in the folds of the cloth. Then the soldier must have met him several times, while walking in circles through the maze of identical streets. He has never come to any boulevard, any broader avenue planted with trees or differing in any way at all from the other streets he has taken. Finally the child had mentioned a few names, the few street names he knew, which were obviously of no use at all.

Now he is knocking his beret sharply against the door jamb in front of which they have both stopped. The interior is brightly lit. A pleated curtain of white, translucent material covers the

lower part of the window that is set in the upper
half of the door. But it is easy for a man of normal height to see the entire room: the bar to
the left, the tables in the middle, a wall on the
right covered with posters of various sizes. There
are few drinkers at this late hour: two workers
sitting at one of the tables and a better-dressed
man standing near the zinc-topped bar over
which the bartender is leaning. The latter is a
thickset man whose size is even more marked
in relation to his customer because of the slightly
raised platform he is standing on. Both men have
simultaneously turned their heads toward the
door where the boy has just knocked his beret
against the jamb.

But they see only the soldier's face above the
curtain. And the child, turning the doorknob
with one hand, again knocks his beret, this time
against the door itself, which is already some
distance from the jamb. The bartender's eyes
have already left the soldier's pale face that is
still silhouetted against the darkness, cut off at
the level of the chin by the curtain, and are
fixed on the widening gap between door and
jamb where the child is about to come in.

As soon as he is inside, the latter turns around
and gestures to the soldier to follow him. This
time everyone stares at the newcomer: the bartender behind his bar, the man dressed in mid-

dle-class clothes standing in front of it, the two workers sitting at a table. One of the two, whose back was to the door, has pivoted on his chair without letting go of his glass that is half full of red wine and set in the middle of the checkered oilcloth. The other glass, just beside the first, is also encircled by a large hand which completely conceals the probable contents. To the left, a ring of reddish liquid indicates another place previously occupied by one of these glasses, or by a third.

Afterwards, it is the soldier himself who is sitting at a table in front of a similar glass, half full of the same dark-colored wine. The glass has left several circular marks on the red-and-white checked oilcloth, but almost all are incomplete, showing a series of more or less closed arcs, occasionally overlapping, almost dry in some places, in others still shiny with the last drops of liquid leaving a film over the blacker deposit already formed, while elsewhere the rings are blurred by being set too close together or even half obliterated by sliding, or else, perhaps, by a quick wipe of a rag.

The soldier, motionless at the foot of his lamp-post, is still waiting, his hands in his overcoat pockets, the same package under his left arm. It is daylight again, the same pale, colorless daylight. But the street light is out now. These are the same apartment houses, the same empty streets, the same gray and white hues, the same cold.

It has stopped snowing. The layer of snow on the ground is scarcely any deeper, perhaps only a little more solidly packed. And the yellowish paths hurrying pedestrians have made along the sidewalks are just the same. On each side of these narrow paths, the white surface has remained virtually intact; tiny changes have nevertheless occurred here and there, for instance the circular area which the soldier's heavy boots have trampled near the lamppost.

It is the child who approaches him this time. At first he is only a vague silhouette, an irregular black spot approaching fairly fast along the outer edge of the sidewalk. Each time this spot passes a street light it makes a sudden movement toward it and immediately continues forward in its original direction. Soon it is easy to make out the agile legs in their narrow black trousers, the black cape billowing out over the shoulders, the beret pulled down over the boy's eyes. Each time the child passes a street light he stretches out his arm toward the cast-iron shaft which his gloved hand grasps while his whole body, with the momentum of its accumulated speed, makes a complete turn around this pivot, his feet scarcely touching the ground until the child is back in his original position on the outer edge of the sidewalk where he continues running forward toward the soldier.

He may not have noticed the latter immediately, for the soldier is partly concealed by the cast-iron shaft his hip and right arm are leaning against. But to get a better look at the boy whose movement is interrupted by pivots and gusts of wind which make his cape billow out each time, the man has stepped forward a little, and the child suddenly stops halfway between the last two lampposts, his feet together, his hands pulling the cape around his rigid body, his alert face with its wide eyes raised toward the soldier.

"Hello," the soldier says.

The child looks at him without surprise, but also without the slightest indication of friendliness, as if he found it both natural and annoying to meet the soldier again.

"Where did you sleep?" he says at last.

The soldier makes a vague gesture with his chin, without bothering to take a hand out of his pocket. "Back there."

"In the barracks?"

"That's right, in the barracks."

The child examines his uniform from head to foot. The greenish overcoat is neither more nor less ragged, the leggings are just as carelessly wrapped, the boots have virtually the same mud stains. But the beard may be a little darker.

"Where is your barracks?"

"Back there," the soldier says. And he repeats the same gesture with his chin, pointing vaguely behind him, or over his right shoulder.

"You don't know how to wrap your leggings," the child says.

The man bends forward slightly and looks down at his boots. "It doesn't matter any more now, you know."

As he straightens up again he notices that the boy is much closer than he expected him to be: only three or four yards away. He did not think the child had come so close to him, nor does he remember having seen him come nearer afterwards. Still, it is hardly likely that the child has changed position without the soldier's knowing it, while the latter's head was down: in so short an interval of time he would scarcely have been able to take a step. Besides, he is standing in exactly the same position as when they first met: stiff in the black cape held shut—even tight, around the body—by his invisible hands, his eyes raised.

"Twelve thousand three hundred forty-five,"

the child says, reading the regimental number on the overcoat collar.

"Yes," the soldier says. "But that isn't my number."

"Yes it is. It's written on you."

"But now, you know . . ."

"It's even written twice." And the child sticks one arm out from under his cape and points his forefinger toward the two red diamond shapes. He is wearing a navy blue sweater and a knitted wool glove the same color.

"All right . . ." the soldier says.

The child puts his arm back under the cape, which he carefully closes again, holding it tight from inside.

"What's in your package?"

"I've already told you."

Suddenly the child turns his head toward the door of the apartment building. Thinking he has seen something unusual there, the soldier turns to look too, but sees only the same vertical dark opening, a hand's width across, separating the door from the jamb. Since the boy is still looking attentively in this direction, the man tries to discern some figure in the shadowy doorway, but without success.

Finally he asks: "What are you looking at?"

"What's in your package?" the child repeats

instead of answering, still not looking away from the open door.

"I've already told you: things."

"What things?"

"My things!"

The boy looks at his interlocutor again:

"You have a knapsack to keep your things in. Every soldier has a knapsack."

He has become increasingly self-assured during the conversation. His voice is now not at all remote, but firm, almost peremptory. The man, on the other hand, speaks lower and lower:

"It's all over now, you know. The war's over . . ."

Again he feels how tired he is. He no longer wants to answer these questions that lead nowhere. He was almost ready to give the boy the package. He looks at the box in its brown wrapping paper under his arm; in drying, the snow has left dark rings on it, their edges fringed with tiny scallops; the string has stretched and slipped toward one of the corners.

The soldier then looks past the still motionless boy down the empty street. Having turned toward the opposite end, he sees the same shallow vista.

"Do you know what time it is?" he asks, resuming his initial position against the cast-iron shaft.

The boy shakes his head several times, from left to right, from right to left.

"Does your father serve meals?"

"He's not my father," the child says; and without giving the man time to ask his question again, he turns on his heel and walks stiffly toward the half-open door. He stops on the doorstep, pushes the door a little farther open, slips into the opening, and closes the door behind him without slamming it but so that the click of the latch falling back into place can nevertheless be clearly heard.

The soldier no longer sees anything in front of him now but the snow-covered sidewalk with its yellowish path on the right side and, to the left, a smooth surface broken by a single, regular set of tracks: two small, widely spaced footprints running parallel to the gutter, then, about four yards from the lamppost, coming together to form an irregular circle before turning at right angles to join the narrower path leading to the apartment house door.

The soldier raises his face toward the gray façade with its rows of uniform windows, a white streak along the bottom of each recess, thinking perhaps he will see the boy appear at one of the windows. But he knows that the child in the cape does not live in this house, for he has already gone with him to where he lives. Besides, judging from the look of the windows, the whole apartment building seems unoccupied.

The heavy red curtains extend across the entire wall from floor to ceiling. The wall opposite them has the chest against it and above that, the picture. The child is where he was, sitting on the floor with his legs folded under him; it looks as if he wants to slide all the way under the bench. But he continues to stare straight ahead, his attention indicated, for want of anything else, by his wide-open eyes.

This sign, of course, is not infallible; if the artist has meant the child to be looking at nothing in particular, if he has imagined no specific feature for the fourth wall of this rectangular room where only three are shown, it could be said that the child is merely staring into space. But in that case, it was not logical to represent him staring at the only one of the four walls that apparently looks out onto something. The three walls shown in the print have, as a matter of fact, no visible opening in them. Even if there is an exit at the left, behind the coat racks, it is certainly not the main entrance to the tavern, whose interior arrangement would then be too out of the ordinary. The main entrance, with white enamel letters spelling out the word "café" and the proprietor's name in two curved lines pasted on the glass in an oval, and below this a pleated curtain of thin, translucent material, obliging anyone who wants to look over it to stand close against the door—this main entrance can be nowhere else but in the wall not shown in the print, the rest of this wall being occupied by a large window, also with a long curtain covering its lower half, and decorated in the middle by three spheres attached to the glass—one red one above two white ones—certainly suggesting that the exit behind the coat racks leads to a poolroom.

The child holding the box in his arms would therefore be looking toward the door. But he is sitting almost at floor level and obviously cannot see the street over the curtain. He is not looking up to see some pale face pressed against the glass, cut off at the level of the neck by the curtain. His gaze is virtually horizontal. Has the door just opened to let in a newcomer who would attract the boy's attention by his unusual attire: a soldier, for instance? This solution seems unlikely, for ordinarily the main entrance is placed next to the bar, that is, in this case, on the far left, where there is a small cleared space in front of the men standing dressed in middle-class clothes. The child, though, is sitting on the right-hand side of the picture, where no passage among the jumble of benches and tables would permit access to the rest of the room.

The soldier, moreover, came in a long time ago. He is sitting at a table, far behind the child, who does not seem at all interested in his uniform. The soldier is also staring straight ahead, his eyes fixed slightly higher; but since he is much farther away from the window than the boy, he need only raise his eyes a few degrees to look through the window above the curtain at the heavily falling snow which again obliterates the footprints, the single set of tracks, the intersecting yellowish paths that run parallel to the high façades.

At the corner of the last apartment house, standing in the L-shaped strip of snow between the latter and the path, his body cut vertically by the angle of the stone, one foot, one leg, one shoulder, and half the black cape out of sight, the boy is on the lookout, his eyes fixed on the cast-iron lamppost. Has he come out of the apartment by another door opening on the cross street? Or has he stepped through a ground floor window? In either case, the soldier pretends not to have noticed his reappearance. Leaning against his street light, he is absorbed in examining the other end of the empty street.

"What are you waiting for?" Then, in the

same tone of voice, after about ten seconds: "What are you waiting for there?"

The voice is certainly the boy's, the tone deliberate, calm, and not friendly, a little too deep for a boy of ten or twelve. But it sounds quite close, scarcely two or three yards away, whereas the corner of the building is at least eight yards off. The man feels like turning around to verify this distance and see if the child has not come closer again. Or else, without looking at him, he might answer his question with the first thing that comes into his head: "The streetcar," or "Christmas," to make the child understand what a bother he is. The soldier continues to stare down the street.

When he finally turns to look at the boy, the latter has completely disappeared. The soldier waits another minute, thinking the boy has only stepped behind the corner of the apartment house and will soon peek out from behind his hiding place. But no such thing happens.

The man looks down at the fresh snow, where the newly made footprints turn at a right angle just in front of him. In the section parallel to the sidewalk the footprints are wide apart and smudged by running, a tiny heap of snow having been thrown up behind each one by the movement of the shoe; on the other hand, the few

footprints leading to the path show the pattern
of the soles very clearly: a series of chevrons
across the width of the sole and, beneath the
heel, a cross inscribed in a circle—that is, on the
heel itself, a cross inscribed in a circular depression in the rubber (a second round hole, much
shallower and of extremely small diameter, perhaps indicating the center of the cross, with the
shoe size shown by figures in relief: thirty-two,
perhaps, thirty-three or thirty-four).

The soldier, who had bent over slightly to
examine the details of the footprints, then walks
to the path. As he does so, he tries to push open
the apartment house door, but the door resists:
it is shut tight. It is a wooden door with ornamental moldings and extremely narrow jambs
on either side. The man continues walking toward the corner of the building and turns down
the cross street, which is as empty as the one
he has just left.

This new route leads him, like the other, to
a right-angle crossroad with a last street light
set some ten yards before the end of the sidewalk and identical façades on each side. The
base of the cast-iron lamppost is a truncated
cone embossed with a strand of ivy, with the
same curves, the same leaves growing at the
same places on the same stems, the same faults

48 /

in the casting. The entire design is accentuated by the snow borders. Perhaps the meeting was supposed to be at this crossroads.

The soldier raises his eyes to look for the enamel plaques which should show the names of these streets. There is nothing visible on one of the stone walls at the corner. On the other, about three yards from the ground, is attached the usual blue plaque, from which the enamel has chipped off in large flakes, as if some boys had relentlessly aimed at it with pebbles; only the word "Rue" is still legible, and, further on, the two letters: ". . . na . . ." followed by a downstroke interrupted by the concentric rings of the next chip. Besides, the original name must have been an extremely short one. The depredations are quite old, for the exposed metal is already badly rusted.

As he is about to cross the street, still following the thin yellow path, to see if he cannot find other street signs in better condition, the man hears a voice quite close by, speaking three or four syllables whose meaning he has not time to grasp. He immediately turns around; but there is no one in sight. In this solitude, the snow probably conducts sound peculiarly.

The voice was low and yet it did not sound like a man's voice . . . A young woman with an extremely low voice—that may have been what it was, but the recollection is too fleeting: already nothing remains but a neutral timbre, without any particular tone; it could belong to anyone, and might not even be a human voice at all. At this moment the soldier notices that the corner apartment house door is not closed. Automatically, he takes a few steps toward it. The interior is so dark that it is impossible to see anything through the gap. To the right, to the left, up above, all the windows are closed, their dirty black panes with neither curtains nor shades suggesting no trace of life in the unlighted rooms, as if the entire building was deserted.

The wooden door has ornamental moldings and is painted dark brown; on either side of the open leaf are the narrow jambs. The soldier pushes the door wide open as he steps up onto the snowy stoop, already covered with footprints, and steps inside.

He is standing at the end of a dark hallway with several doors opening off it. At the other end can be seen the beginning of a staircase that soon vanishes in the darkness. The end of this long narrow hallway opens onto another hallway perpendicular to it, indicated by even darker shadows on each side of the staircase.

The hallway is empty, without any of those household objects that generally suggest the existence of life: door mats in front of the doors, toys left at the foot of the stairs, a bucket and mop in a corner. Here there is nothing, except the floor and the walls; and even the walls are bare, all painted some very dark color; immediately to the left of the entrance is tacked the small white civil defense bulletin instructing the residents what to do in case of fire. The floor is made of wood blackened by mud and slops, as are the first steps—the only ones clearly visible—of the staircase. After five or six steps the staircase seems to turn to the right. The soldier can now make out the wall behind the stairs. Here, flattened against the wall, her arms held stiffly at her side, there is a woman in a full skirt with a long apron tied around her waist; she is staring at the open door and the figure standing in it, silhouetted against the light.

Before the man has had time to speak to her, a door on the left side of the hallway suddenly opens, and another woman in an apron, heavier-set than the first and perhaps older too, steps out. Looking up, she stops short, opens her mouth wide—too wide—and as she steps back into her doorway begins to scream, the shrill sound rising until it comes to an end with the violent slamming of her door. At the same moment comes the sound of hurried footsteps going up the staircase; it is the other woman running away, vanishing at once, the pounding of her clogs continuing without slowing down, but fading from floor to floor as she climbs, her full skirt, billowing around her legs, perhaps held down with one hand, not even stopping on the landings to catch her breath, the only clue as to her position being suggested by a different resonance at the beginning and the end of each flight: one floor, two floors, three or four floors, or even more.

Afterwards there is complete silence again. But, on the right side of the hallway this time, another door has opened. Or was it already open before? It is more likely that the sudden uproar has just attracted this new figure, which resembles the preceding two, or at least the first: a woman, also young, apparently, and wearing a long dark-gray apron tied around her waist and hanging full around her hips. Her eyes having met the soldier's, she asks:

"What's going on?"

Her voice is low, deep, but without any intonation; there is a premeditated quality about it, as if she wanted to sound as impersonal as possible. This might also be the voice heard in the street a moment ago.

"They got scared," the soldier says.

"Yes," the woman says, "it's from seeing you standing there like that . . . with the light behind you . . . they can't see . . . they thought you were a . . ."

She does not finish her sentence. She stands still, staring at him. She opens her door no wider, probably feeling safer inside, one hand resting on the jamb, the other holding the door, ready to close it again. She asks:

"What do you want?"

"I'm looking for a street . . ." the soldier says, "A street I have to go to."

"What street?"

"That's just it. I can't remember the name. It was something like Galavier, or Matadier. But I'm not sure. Could it be Montoret?"

The woman seems to be thinking.

"This is a big city, you know," she says at last.

"But it's around here somewhere, that's what they told me."

The young woman turns her head toward the interior of the apartment and in a louder voice questions someone who remains invisible: "Did you ever hear of a Rue Montoret? Somewhere near here? Or something that sounds like that?"

She waits for the answer, revealing her regular profile as she turns toward the open door.

Everything behind her is dark: there must be a hallway without any windows. The heavy-set woman also came out of complete darkness. After a moment a faint voice answers a few indistinct words, and the young woman turns back toward the soldier:

"Wait here a minute. I'll go see."

She begins to close the door, then changes her mind: "Close the street door," she says, "the whole house is getting cold."

The soldier walks back to the door and pushes it shut, the latch making a faint click as it falls back into place. He is in the dark again. The woman's door must be closed too. It is not even possible to walk toward it, for there is no means of recognizing anything, not even a gleam of light. Complete darkness. Nor can the slightest sound be heard: neither steps nor murmurs nor the clatter of kitchen utensils. The whole house seems uninhabited. The soldier closes his eyes and again sees the white flakes falling slowly, the row of street lights at regular intervals from one end of the snow-covered sidewalk to the other, and the boy running away as fast as he can, appearing and disappearing, visible each time for a few seconds in the successive circles of light at equal intervals of time, though the space is increasingly foreshortened by the distance, so that the boy seems to be running slower and slower as he grows smaller and smaller.

It is six steps from the chest to the table: three steps to the fireplace and three more after that. It is five steps from the table to the corner of the bed; four steps from the bed to the chest. The path from the chest to the table is not quite straight: it swerves slightly in order to pass closer to the fireplace. Above the fireplace is a mirror, a large rectangular mirror fastened to the wall. The foot of the bed is directly opposite.

Suddenly the light reappears in the hallway. It is not the same light, and it does not directly illuminate the place where the soldier is standing, which remains in darkness. At the other end of the hallway, a pale yellow artificial light comes from the right side of the transverse hallway. A luminous rectangle thus appears against the far right wall just in front of the staircase, and the illuminated area begins to widen from there, tracing two oblique lines across the floor: one of which crosses the blackened flooring of the hallway, the other rising diagonally up the first three steps; beyond the latter, as on this side of the former, the darkness remains, though slightly reduced.

Also on the right, in the area which cannot be seen, where the light is coming from, a door closes gently and a key turns in a lock. Then the lights go out and it is dark again. But footsteps, probably guided by long familiarity with the premises, are advancing down the transverse hallway. They are regular, distinct footsteps which do not hesitate. They advance down the hallway in front of the staircase opposite the soldier who, in order to avoid the collision of two bodies in the darkness, gropes blindly around him, looking for a wall against which he can flatten himself. But the footsteps are not heading toward him: instead of turning into the hallway at the end of which he is standing, they have continued straight ahead, into the left branch of the transverse hallway. A bolt is drawn and a harsher light, from outside, appears in this left section of the hallway, its intensity increasing until it becomes a kind of dim gray twilight. There must be another outside door here, opening onto the other street. It is through this door that the boy would have gone out again. Soon the light disappears as it had come, gradually, and the door closes at the same time that complete darkness is re-established.

Darkness. Click. Yellow light. Click. Darkness. Click. Gray light. Click. Darkness. And the footsteps echoing across the hallway floor. And the footsteps echoing across the pavement, in the snow-covered street. And the snow beginning to fall. And the boy's intermittent figure growing smaller and smaller in the distance, from street light to street light.

If the last person had not left by the same door as the boy, but from this side of the building, he would have let daylight into this part of the hallway as he opened the door, and discovered the soldier pressed against the wall, suddenly appearing in broad daylight a few inches away. As in the case of a collision in the darkness, new screams might then have aroused the whole house a second time, sending shadows scampering toward the staircase and bringing terrified faces to half-open doors, necks craning, eyes anxious, mouths already opening to shout . . .

"There is no Rue Montalet around here, nothing like that," the low voice announces; and immediately afterwards: "You're standing in the dark! You should have turned on the light." At these words the light comes on in the hallway, yellow light from a naked bulb on a wire from the ceiling, illuminating the young woman in a gray apron whose arm is still extended outside her doorway; her hand resting on the white porcelain switch moves downward while her pale eyes are fixed on the man, shifting from his hol-

4

low cheeks where the beard is almost a quarter
of an inch long to the box wrapped in brown
paper and the clumsily wrapped leggings, then
moving back to the drawn features of his face.
"You're tired," she says.

It is not a question. The voice has again become neutral, low, without intonation, cautious
perhaps. The soldier makes a vague gesture with
his free hand; a half-smile twists one corner of his
mouth.

"You're not wounded, are you?"

His free hand rises a little higher: "No, no,"
the man says. "I'm not wounded." And his hand
falls back slowly. Then they stand there for a
while looking at each other without speaking.

"What are you going to do," the woman
finally asks, "since you can't find the name of
that street?"

"I don't know," the soldier says.

"Was it for something important?"

"Yes . . . No . . . Probably."

After another silence, the young woman asks
again: "What was it?"

"I don't know," the soldier says. He is tired,
he wants to sit down, anywhere, here, against
the wall. Mechanically he repeats: "I don't
know."

"You don't know what you were going to do
there?"

"I have to go there to find out."

"Oh! . . ."

"I was supposed to meet someone. Now it's too late."

During this dialogue, the woman has opened her door wide and stepped forward in the opening. She is wearing a long black dress with a full skirt, the latter three-quarters hidden by a gray pleated apron tied around her waist. The bottom of the apron is extremely full, like the skirt, while the top is merely a simple square of material protecting the front of her dress. Her face has regular, strongly marked features. Her hair is black. But her eyes are pale, a color between blue-green and gray-blue. She does not avoid the soldier's eyes, but instead stares at him for a long time, though without permitting the soldier to determine what her attitude toward him is.

"You haven't eaten," she says. And a fleeting nuance, as though of pity or fear or surprise, can be detected in her words this time.

But as soon as she has spoken her sentence and silence has fallen again, it becomes impossible to recapture the intonation which seemed just now to have a meaning—fear, boredom, doubt, solicitude, some sort of interest—and all that remains is the declaration: "You haven't eaten," pronounced in a neutral tone of voice. The man repeats his evasive gesture.

"Come in for a minute," she says, perhaps reluctantly—or perhaps not.

Click. Darkness. Click. Yellow light, now illuminating a tiny vestibule where there is a coat rack covered with hats and coats. Click. Darkness.

Now a door opens into a square room furnished with a day bed, a rectangular table, and a marble-topped chest. The table is covered with a red-and-white checked oilcloth. A fireplace with cold ashes in an open grate but without andirons on the hearth occupies the center of one wall. To the right of this fireplace is another door, ajar, opening into a dark room or closet.

"Here," the young woman says, pointing to a wicker chair beside the table, "sit down." The soldier shifts the chair slightly, grasping it at the top of its back, and sits down. He rests his right forearm and hand on the oilcloth. His left hand has remained in his overcoat pocket, the left arm still holding the box wrapped in brown paper at his side.

In the opening of the door, but one or two feet away, the figure of a child stands motionless, turned toward the man in uniform whom his mother (is it his mother?) has just brought into the apartment and who is sitting obliquely at the table, half-leaning on the red oilcloth, his shoulders hunched, his head bent forward.

The woman returns through the door to the vestibule. In one hand she is holding at her waist a piece of bread and a glass. Her other arm hangs at her side and in that hand she is holding a bottle by the neck. She sets everything down on the table in front of the soldier.

Without speaking she fills the glass to the brim. Then she leaves the room again. The bottle is an ordinary liter of colorless glass, half full of dark-red wine; the glass, which is in front of it, near the man's hand, is of coarse manufacture, the shape of a cylindrical goblet, fluted for half its height. The bread is to the left: the heel of a large black loaf whose cross-section is a half-circle with rounded corners; the loaf has a close texture with extremely small, evenly spaced holes. The man's hand is red, injured by rough work and the cold; the outer surface of the fingers, which are folded toward the palm, reveals many tiny crevices at the joints; they are, moreover, stained black, as though by grease, which might have adhered to the chapped areas of the skin so that a perfunctory washing would not have made them clean. Hence the bony protuberance at the base of the forefinger is criss-crossed with short black lines, mostly parallel or only slightly divergent, the others variously oriented, surrounding the first lines or cutting across them.

Above the fireplace a large rectangular mirror is fastened to the wall; the wall reflected in it is the one with the large chest against the base of it. In the middle of this wall is the full-length photograph of a soldier in battle dress—perhaps the husband of the young woman with the low voice and the pale eyes, and perhaps the father of the child. Overcoat with front flaps folded back, leggings, heavy boots: the uniform is that of the infantry, as is the chin-strapped helmet and the full equipment of knapsack, canteen, belt, cartridge belt, etc. The man's hands are closed, one a little above his belt, over the two leather straps that cross each other over his chest; he has a carefully trimmed moustache; the figure as a whole, moreover, has a neat, almost lacquered quality, doubtless due to the skillful retouching of the specialist who has made this enlargement; the face itself, wearing the usual smile, has been so smoothed, scratched out, and rearranged that it no longer has any character at all, resembling all those faces of soldiers or sailors about to go into battle displayed in photographers' windows. Yet the original snapshot seems to have been taken by an amateur—probably the young woman or some friend

in the regiment—for the setting is not that of a
fake middle-class living room nor of a false ter-
race lined with potted palms in front of a park
painted in *trompe-l'oeil* on canvas, but the street
itself in front of the apartment house door near
the street light with the conical shaft around
which curls a spray of stylized ivy.

The man's equipment is brand new. The
photograph must date from the beginning of
the war, the period of general mobilization, or
from the first draft of reservists, perhaps even
from a date previous to this: during military
service or a brief training period. Yet the full
paraphernalia of the soldier in battle dress seems
rather to indicate that the photograph dates from
the beginning of the war itself, for the infantry-
man on leave in peacetime does not come home
in such uncomfortable garb. Hence the most
likely occasion would be an exceptional leave
of a few hours, granted to the draftee to say
goodbye to his family before starting for the
front. No friend in the regiment came with him,
for the young woman would then be in the photograph beside the soldier; she must have taken
the photograph with her own camera; she has
even probably devoted a whole roll of film to
the occasion, and she has later had the best
picture enlarged.

The man is standing outside, in full sunlight,

because there is not enough light inside the apartment; he has simply stepped outside his door and decided to stand near the lamppost. In order to be facing the source of light, he has turned in the direction of the street, having behind him on the right (that is, on his left) the stone corner of the building; the street light on his other side is brushed by the bottom of his overcoat. The soldier glances at his feet and for the first time notices the spray of ivy embossed on the cast iron. The five-lobed, pointed palmate leaves with their five projecting veins are growing on a rather long stem; at the point where each of them joins it, this stem changes direction, but the alternating curves it thus describes are scarcely evident on one side, and on the other are quite pronounced, which gives the entire stem a generally concave movement, preventing the spray from reaching very high and allowing it to curl around the cone; then it divides in two, and the upper branch, which is shorter and has only three leaves growing on it (of which the one at the tip is extremely small), rises in a blunted sine-curve; the other branch disappears toward the opposite side of the cone and the edge of the sidewalk. Once the roll of film is used up the soldier returns to the apartment house.

The hallway is dark, as usual. The apartment

door has remained ajar; he pushes it open, crosses the unlighted vestibule, and sits down at the table where his wife pours him some wine. He drinks without saying anything, taking small mouthfuls, each time setting down the glass on the checkered oilcloth. After many repetitions of this action, the area in front of him is entirely covered with circular stains, though almost all of them are incomplete, showing a series of more or less closed arcs, occasionally overlapping, almost dry in some places, in others still shiny with the last drops of liquid. Between mouthfuls of wine, the soldier keeps his eyes fixed on this confused network which becomes increasingly complicated from moment to moment. He does not know what to say. He should be going now. But when he has finished his glass, the woman pours him another; and he drinks it too, in small mouthfuls, while slowly eating the rest of the bread. The child's silhouette he had noticed in the half-open door to the next room has disappeared in the darkness.

When the soldier decides to look up at the young woman, she is sitting opposite him: not at the table, but on a chair placed (has she just put it there?) in front of the chest, under the black frame of the portrait fastened to the wall. She is examining her visitor's faded uniform; her gray eyes move up as far as his neck where the two pieces of red felt marked with his serial number are sewn.

"What regiment is that?" she asks finally with an upward movement of her chin to indicate the two bright-red diamonds.

"I don't know," the soldier says.

This time the woman shows a certain amount of surprise. "You've forgotten the name of your regiment too?"

"No, that's not it . . . But this overcoat isn't mine." The young woman remains where she is for a moment without speaking. Yet she seems to have a question on her mind which she doesn't know how to formulate or which she hesitates to ask directly. Then, after a whole minute's silence, or even more, she asks: "Whose was it?"

"I don't know," the soldier says.

Besides, if he had known he could probably also have said what regiment the bright-red diamonds represented. Again he looks at the photographic enlargement hanging on the wall above the woman's black hair. The picture is oval-shaped, blurred around the edges; the mat around it has remained creamy-white all the way to the rectangular frame of dark wood. At this distance, the distinguishing insignia are not visible on the overcoat collar. In any case the uniform is that of the infantry. The man must have been billeted in the city or in its immediate environs while waiting to be sent to the front; otherwise he could not have come to say good-bye to his wife before leaving. But where are the barracks in this city? Are there a lot of them? What units are billeted there in peacetime?

The soldier decides he ought to show an interest in these matters: they would provide a normal and harmless subject of conversation. But he has scarcely opened his mouth when he notices a change in the woman's attitude. She is squinting slightly as she looks at him, seeming to wait for the rest of his words with exaggeratedly strained attention, considering the importance he himself attaches to them. He pulls up short in the middle of a vague sentence hurriedly concluded in a direction its inception did not suggest; its interrogative character is so faint that the woman has every opportunity to refrain from answering. And in fact this is the solution she adopts. But her features remain tense. Such questions are obviously the very ones a clumsy spy would ask, and suspicion is natural under such circumstances . . . although it is rather late, now, to conceal the location of military objectives from the enemy.

The soldier has finished his bread and his wine. He has no further reason to linger in this apartment, in spite of his desire to enjoy a few moments more of this relative warmth, this uncomfortable chair, and this guarded presence facing him. He should think up some way of leaving gracefully which would reduce the impression left by the recent misunderstanding. In any case, trying to justify himself would be the worst mistake of all; and how explain convincingly his ignorance about . . . The soldier now tries to remember the exact words he has just used. There was the word "barracks," but he cannot recall the strange sentence he has spoken; he is not even certain he has actually referred to the location of the buildings and still less whether he has definitely indicated that he was not familiar with it.

Without realizing it, he may have passed in front of a barracks during his peregrinations. However he has not noticed any structure in the usual barracks style: a low building (only two floors, with identical windows framed in red brick) about a hundred yards long with a low-pitched slate roof surmounted by high rectangular chimneys also made of brick. The structure rises at the far end of a large, bare, gravel courtyard separated from the boulevard and its luxuriant trees by a high iron fence supported by abutments and bristling with pickets on the inside as well as toward the street. Sentry boxes, placed at intervals, shelter armed guards; these sentry boxes are made of wood, with zinc roofs, and each side is painted with large black and red chevrons.

The soldier has seen nothing of the kind. He has passed along no fence; he has not noticed any large gravel courtyard; he has encountered neither luxuriant foliage nor sentry boxes, nor of course any armed guards. He has not even walked down any tree-lined boulevards. He has always followed only the same straight streets between two high rows of flat housefronts; but a barracks might also look like these. The sentry boxes have been removed, of course, as well as anything that might distinguish the building from those on either side; there remain only the iron bars protecting the first-floor windows for most of their height. These are square vertical bars a hand's breadth apart, connected by two horizontal bars placed not far from each end. The upper ends of these vertical bars are free, terminating in points about eight inches from the top of the window recess; the bases of the bars must be set in the stone sill, but this detail is not visible because of the snow which has drifted there, forming an irregular layer across the entire horizontal surface, particularly thick on the right side.

But this might just as well be a fire house, or a convent, or a school, or an office building, or merely an apartment house whose first-floor windows are protected by iron bars. Having reached the next crossroad, the soldier turns at right angles into the adjoining street.

And the snow continues falling—slow, vertical, uniform—and the white layer thickens imperceptibly on the windowsills, on the doorsteps, on the projecting parts of the black lampposts, on the street without traffic, on the deserted sidewalks where the paths made by pedestrians during the course of the day have already disappeared. And it is night once again.

The regular flakes, all the same size, equally spaced, fall at the same rate of speed, maintaining the same distance between themselves and the same arrangements, as if they belonged to the same rigid system which shifts position from top to bottom with a continuous, vertical, uniform, and slow movement.

The footprints of the straggling pedestrian walking head down in front of the houses, from one end of the straight street to the other, appear one by one in the smooth, fresh snow into which they already sink at least a half an inch. And behind him, the snow immediately begins covering up the prints of his hobnail boots, gradually reconstituting the original whiteness of the trampled area, soon restoring its granular, velvety, fragile appearance, blurring the sharp crests of its edges, making its outlines more and more fluid, and at last entirely filling the depression, so that the difference in level becomes indistinguishable from that of the adjoining areas, continuity then being re-established so that the entire surface is again smooth, intact, untouched.

Hence the soldier cannot know if someone else has passed along here, in front of the houses with their unlighted windows, some time before him. And when he reaches the next crossroad, no tracks appear along the sidewalks of the cross street, and this means nothing either.

However the boy's footprints take longer to disappear. In fact he leaves humps behind him as he runs: his sole, shifting sharply, accumulates a tiny heap of snow which then remains in the middle of the footprint (at the place where its outline is narrowest) whose more or less accentuated protuberance must take longer to efface than the rest; and the holes made on each side of the shoe's toe and heel are all the deeper since the boy does not follow the old paths made during the day, but prefers to walk near the edge of the sidewalk in the deeper snow (though no difference in depth is apparent to the eye), where he sinks in farther. Since, in addition, he proceeds very rapidly, from the point where he is to the last irregularity still discernible under the new layer of snow, the length of his course is much greater than that the soldier leaves behind him, particularly if the loops which punctuate the child's progress around each lamppost are included.

These loops, it is true, are not indicated with absolute clarity, for the child scarcely sets foot on the ground during the revolution he makes as he catches hold of the cast-iron shaft. As for the pattern of his rubber-soled shoes, it is already blurred: neither the chevrons nor the cross in the center of its circle are identifiable, even before the falling snow has begun to blur the image. The distortions produced by running, added to the uncertainty concerning the latter's characteristics, make it impossible, all in all, to differentiate these footprints from those left by another child of the same age—who would also be wearing, moreover, shoes with identical soles (the same shoes, perhaps, coming from the same store) and who would be making similar loops around the lampposts.

In any case, there are no tracks at all in the snow, no footprints, and the snow continues falling over the empty street, uniform, vertical, and slow. It must be entirely dark now, and the flakes are no longer visible except when they fall through the zone of light around a street light.

Hence the street is punctuated at regular intervals (though these seem to grow increasingly
shorter in proportion to their distance to the right
or the left), punctuated with lighter zones where
the darkness is stippled with innumerable tiny
white particles animated with a common falling
movement. Since the window is located on the
top floor, all these circles of light must look pale
and distant at the bottom of the long trench
formed by the two parallel planes of the housefronts; so distant, in fact, so quivering, that it
is naturally impossible to tell the flakes apart:
seen from so high up they form at intervals only
a vague whitish halo, itself dim because the light
from the street lamps is extremely weak and
made still more uncertain by the diffused reflection which all these pale surfaces spread around
them—the earth, the sky, the curtain of close
flakes falling slowly but without interruption in
front of the windows, so thick that it now completely conceals the building opposite, the cast-
iron street lights, the last straggling pedestrian,
the entire street.

Perhaps even the street lights have not been
turned on this evening, tonight, that night. As
for the sound of possible footsteps, muffled by
the fresh snow, it could not reach such an alti-
tude, penetrate the iron shutters, the window-
panes, the thick velvet curtains.

The shadow of the fly on the ceiling has stopped near the place where the circle cast by the lampshade meets the top of the red curtain. Once it is motionless, the shape becomes more complex. It is indeed the enlarged reproduction of the bent filament of the electric bulb, but the primary image is repeated nearby by two other paler, vaguer images framing the first. Perhaps, too, still other less distinct images are further multiplied on each side of the latter; they are not perceptible, for the whole of the tiny figure the fly projects is not situated in the most brightly illuminated area of the ceiling, but in a fringe of half-light about a quarter of an inch wide bordering the entire periphery of the circle, at the edge of the shadow.

All the rest of the room, lighted by only this one lamp on the corner of the table, seems to be in relative darkness compared to the brilliant circle of light cast on the white ceiling. Eyes which have stared too long at the latter no longer make out, when they turn away, any detail on the room's other walls. The picture hanging on the rear wall is nothing more than a gray rectangle framed in black; the chest beneath it is nothing more than a dark square as flat as the picture, pasted there like a piece of wallpaper; and the same is true for the fireplace in the center of the perpendicular wall. As for the wallpaper itself, the innumerable tiny spots which constitute its pattern look no more like a torch than a flower, a human figure, a dagger, a street light, or anything. The wallpaper merely looks as if silent feathers were falling in regular lines at a uniform rate, so slowly that their movement is scarcely noticeable, and it is difficult to decide whether their direction is up or down, like particles suspended in motionless water, tiny bubbles in a gaseous liquid, snowflakes, dust. And on the floor, which is also in semi-darkness, the gleaming paths have disappeared.

Only the table top under the conical lampshade is illuminated, as is the bayonet lying in the center. Its short heavy blade with two symmetrical edges reveals, on either side of the central axis, two symmetrically sloping planes of polished steel, one of which reflects the lamplight toward the middle of the room.

On the other side of the room, in the middle of the wall, the picture obscured by the darkness is nothing more than a gray oval within a vertical white rectangle, the latter framed in black.

At this moment a faint voice is heard, quite close, indistinct. The soldier lowers his gaze from the picture of the soldier fastened to the wall to the young woman sitting on her chair in front of the chest. But the voice heard just now is not hers; as low perhaps and not so young, it was

certainly a man's voice this time. Besides, it is
repeating a sentence of approximately the same
sound, still just as incomprehensible, while the
young woman remains bolt upright in her chair,
her mouth closed, her eyes turned toward the
corner of the room where the open door is, on
the other side of the table. The dark area separating the open door from its jamb reveals nothing in the next room.

The young woman is now standing in front
of this door which she has pushed farther open,
wide enough to slip through it; then the door
is pushed back without closing altogether, keeping the same open space as before. In the dark
area which remains, the child then reappears.

At least a vertical strip of the child then reappears, consisting of an eye, the nose, three-
quarters of the mouth and the chin, an elongated
rectangle of blue smock, half a bare knee, a sock,
a black felt slipper, remaining rigid while the
man's voice repeats its same sentence for the
third time, not so loud, which again keeps any
sound from being recognized except the tenta-
tive noises that have no meaning. The woman's
low voice answers, still more softly, almost in a
whisper. The child's eye is on a level with the
doorknob, a white porcelain oval. On the other
side, an electric light switch also made out of
porcelain is set in the wall near the jamb. An

argument is going on; the young woman speaks more rapidly, giving long explanations in which the same groups of words with the same intonations seem to recur several times. The man's voice intervenes only in short sentences, or even in monosyllables, if not in snarls and grunts. The child, growing bolder, opens the door a little wider.

No, it is not the child, instead the child disappears, replaced by the young woman whose head appears a little higher in the widened opening: "It wasn't Boulard, was it?" And since the soldier looks at her questioningly, she repeats, "Rue Boulard? That isn't what you were looking for?"

"No . . . I don't think so . . ." the soldier says in an uncertain tone of voice. Then, after a moment's thought, with a little more assurance, he shakes his head several times from right to left: "I don't think so. No." But his interlocutor is already no longer there; and now the door has been shut tight.

The white oval knob shows several shining points; the brightest point is located at the very top; another, much larger but less brilliant, makes a kind of curvilinear four-sided polygon on the right side. Bright lines of various widths, lengths, and intensities follow the general contour of the rounded surface at varying distances like those customarily represented in drawings to simulate relief.

But these concentric lines, instead of according the object a third dimension, seem to make it revolve: by staring at it continuously, the soldier can see the porcelain knob move, first scarcely perceptibly, then with increasing amplitude, the axis of the oval alternately tilting ten or twenty degrees to either side of the vertical. Nevertheless the door does not open. But perhaps the child, on the other side, is playing with the handle, with the other white porcelain handle identical with this one and symmetrically placed in relation to the plane of the door.

When the door opens again, it admits neither the timid and curious child nor the young woman with pale eyes, but someone new: doubtless the person who was speaking in the next room just now; it is, in fact, a voice of similar timbre and volume which is now assuring the soldier that there is no Rue Boucharet in either this neighborhood or the whole city for that matter. It must have been "Boulard" that he heard; and the man offers to explain where this street is. "It's not very near!" he adds, examining the soldier sitting in his chair, his hands lying flat on his thighs, his back a little hunched, the battered package still tucked under his arm, scrutinizing him with an insistence which seems to be cal-

culating the number of miles he is still capable
of covering before collapsing for good.

The man himself is well within draft age, but
he is lame, which explains his presence among
civilians. His left leg seems unusable; he walks
with the help of a wooden crutch under one arm-
pit, using it skillfully, judging by the swift maneuver he has just made in order to come into
the room and approach the table, on the edge
of which his right hand is now resting, on the
red-and-white checked oilcloth. Perhaps he is a
war casualty: he might have been wounded at
the beginning of hostilities and been sent home
on foot despite his condition, before the retreat
of the defeated armies and the evacuation of
the military hospitals. He has a thin, carefully
trimmed moustache, like the soldier in the photograph. As a matter of fact, he might resemble
the latter quite closely, at least as much as a
picture of that kind, after so much retouching,
can resemble its model. But a picture of that
kind, in fact, proves nothing. The soldier shakes
his head several times to indicate his disagreement: "No," he answers, "it didn't sound like
Bouchard."

"I said Bouvard."

"I don't think so. No, it was something else."

"There is nothing else."

"Besides it was around here."

"Then you know the city?"

"No . . . but it's . . ."

"Well if you don't know your way, how can you tell? I know this city. My leg hasn't always been like this . . ." With his chin he indicates his crutch. "Your Rue Bouvard is at the other end of town!"

The soldier is prepared to explain his reasons for being sure of the contrary, or, more exactly, for thinking that the street he is looking for is not the Rue Bouvard, but without going into complicated details it will be difficult for him to convince the invalid who, on his part, shows so much assurance. Besides, on reflection, his own reasons already seem less convincing to him. And he is about to resign himself to listening to the information the other man is so insistent on giving him, when the young woman also returns through the door which has remained ajar. She seems displeased. She comes in hurriedly, as if she had been delayed by a sudden, urgent task which has prevented her from accompanying the man a few moments before, or even from keeping him out of the visitor's sight.

The lame man has begun his topographical explanations in which a number of street names figure: Vanizier, Vantardier, Bazaman, Davidson, Tamani, Duroussel, Dirbonne, etc. The young woman interrupts him in the middle of his itinerary: "But he already told you it wasn't Broulard."

"Not Broulard: Bouvard! I know just where it is." And, turning toward the soldier as if he were in no doubt of the answer: "You're going to the warehouse?"

"The warehouse?"

"Yes: the military warehouse, the one they've been using as an auxiliary barracks."

"No," the soldier says, "it's not a barracks I'm looking for, and not a warehouse either."

"Well, barracks or not, that doesn't change where the street is." Suddenly getting an idea, he drums his fingertips on the table and speaks to the woman: "Let the boy take him there, that would be easiest."

Without changing her adamant expression, she shrugs her shoulders as she answers: "You know I don't want him to go out."

A new argument begins between them, if it was the same man the first time. Contrary, in any case, to the dialogue which took place in the next room, it is now the man who does most of the talking, asking for precise reasons why the child should be shut up, scarcely listening to the answers, repeating peremptorily that no one runs any danger crossing the city, especially a child, that it will not take him long anyway, that it will not even be dark by the time he gets back. The woman answers him with short, irritated, insistent sentences: "You just said it was far away."

"Far away for someone who doesn't know where it is. But not for the boy, he'll get there by the shortest route and come back again right away."

"I'd rather he didn't go out," the young woman says.

This time the man calls the visitor to witness: what danger would there be in going out today? Aren't the streets absolutely calm? Could anything happen before nightfall? . . . etc.

The soldier answers that he doesn't know. As for the streets being calm, for the moment it is certainly incontestable.

"But they might come any minute," the woman says.

The lame man does not agree with her: "Not before tomorrow night," he declares, "or even the day after. Otherwise do you think he'd just be standing here waiting for them?" He is referring to the soldier now, with a broad, vague gesture in his direction, across the table; but the latter personally does not find the argument very convincing, for he should not be here in any case.

When the man appeals to him again, he can only
make an evasive gesture with his hand which he
barely lifts from his knee:

"I don't know," he says.

Besides, he is not at all eager to be taken
to the other side of town, although he no longer
knows now what else he could do. Far from feeling rested by this pause, an even greater lassi-
tude has now come over him. He looks at the
young woman with her pale eyes, her set face,
her black hair, her wide apron tied around her
waist; he looks at the lame man whose infirmity
does not seem to tire him, since he remains standing, supported by his crutch, although there is
an empty chair nearby; the soldier wonders
whether his useless leg is resting on the floor,
but he cannot tell, for the man, leaning on the
other end of the table, is visible only above the
thighs: he would therefore have to lean forward,
raise the edge of the oilcloth, and look under the
table, between the four square legs that taper
toward the bottom—or else, tapering toward the
bottom, but made out of turned, fluted wood,
becoming cylindrical and smooth at the upper
end, terminating at the top in four cubes with a
carved rose on two of their sides—or else . . . ;
the soldier looks again at the portrait on the rear
wall: at this distance, the features of the face are
quite indistinct; as for the details of the uniform,

they would have to be already familiar in order
to be visible: the two straps crossing each other
over the chest, the dagger-bayonet with its black
leather sheath attached to the belt, the overcoat
with its front flaps folded back, the leggings . . .
unless the latter are puttees, or even boots . . .

But now the child is coming in to the left of
the chest, through the vestibule door. He is being
pushed forward toward the soldier who is still
sitting at the table. It is the lame man who
pushes him from behind with his free hand while
the crutch makes tiny quick movements in virtually the same place, for the boy does not move
forward. The wounded leg is slightly shorter
than the other one, or else slightly bent, so that
the foot hangs about an inch or so above the
floor.

The child has changed clothes, probably to
go outside: he is now wearing long narrow
trousers, out of which appear his high shoes, and
a heavy wool turtleneck sweater that comes
down to the hips; a cape, not closed, hangs from
his shoulders to his knees; his head is covered
with a beret pulled down on each side over his
ears. Everything is of the same navy blue color,
or, more exactly, of the various shades associated
with this color.

The lame man having exerted a firmer pres-
sure on the child's back, the latter advances a

step towards the soldier; at the same time he draws tight the two flaps of his cape, holding the edges with both hands from the inside. Then the man speaks a sentence already heard a few seconds before: "He'll find your Rue Bouvard for you, he'll find it." The child stubbornly looks down at his heavy shoes whose rubber soles are a yellow line on the floor.

Has the woman finally given in? Yet the soldier has not noticed that she has given her consent, in his presence, for the child to go out. Had this scene taken place out of his sight? But where and when? Or was her consent not being considered? She is standing a little to one side, in the shadowy frame of the wide-open door. She is motionless, her arms hanging stiffly at her sides. She says nothing, but she has probably just said something, which might have attracted the soldier's attention in this direction. Her clothes too have been changed: she no longer wears an apron over her full gray skirt. Her face retains the same hostile expression, though perhaps it is gentler, more remote now. Her eyes are larger in the darkness; she looks across the table, where the empty glass is set, at the child, himself motionless in the dark cape which completely conceals him from neck to knees; the location of his invisible hands inside the cape is indicated at two different levels near the neck and toward

the middle of the cape by a gathering of the edge
of the material. Behind the child, the man with
the crutch has also stopped moving entirely; he
is leaning forward, his back bent, his balance,
which seems precarious, made possible by the
crutch held obliquely to support his body and
firmly grasped in his hand, his arm extended,
his shoulder high, his other free arm moving
forward toward the boy's back, his hand partly
open, his forefinger and middle finger almost
straight while the other two are closed over the
palm which is turned upward. The expression on
his face has frozen into a kind of smile, a "kind
smile" perhaps, that the stiffness of the features
transforms, however, into a grimace: one corner
of the mouth twisted, one eye more nearly closed
than the other, and the cheek half contracted.

"He'll find your Rue Bouvard for you, he'll
find it."

No one says anything. The child looks at his
shoes. The lame man's body is still leaning forward as though about to fall, his right arm half
extended, his mouth distorted by what was a
smile. The woman seems to have stepped back
still farther into the shadow of the next room,
and her eyes look still larger, fixed now, perhaps,
on the soldier.

And afterwards there is the street, the night,
the falling snow. The soldier, hugging his pack-

age under his arm, his hands thrust into his overcoat pockets, laboriously follows the boy who is three or four yards ahead of him. The tiny dense flakes are driven horizontally by the wind, and the soldier, in order not to receive them full in the face, bends his head down farther; he also squints as much as he can without closing his eyes completely. He can scarcely see, vanishing and reappearing at the bottom of the overcoat, the two black shoes which alternately advance and retreat over the snow.

When he passes through the light of a street light, he sees the tiny white specks rushing toward him, quite distinct against the dark leather of his shoes, and, higher up, clinging to the material of his overcoat. Since he is then illuminated himself, he tries to raise his head at that moment in order to catch a glimpse of the boy in front of him. But the latter, of course, has already vanished into the darkness; and the many white flakes interposed between them are, on the contrary, illuminated by the street light, which prevents anything outside the zone of light from being distinguished. Soon blinded by the tiny crystals which whip against his face, the soldier must lower his eyes again to the overcoat, which is gradually being covered with snow, the badly tied package, and the heavy boots which continue their alternating movement like two pendulums making parallel, identical oscillations side by side but in the opposite directions.

It is only a few steps farther on, once out of the circle of light, that he can again ascertain the boy's presence, a wavering shadow, the cape fluttering in the wind against the bright background of the next street lamp, five or six yards ahead.

And the child has disappeared for good. The soldier is alone, standing stock still. This is a street like the others. The child has brought him here and left him alone, in front of a house like the others, and has told him: "It's here." The soldier has looked at the house, the street, from one side and then from the other, and the door. It was a door like the others. The street was long and black with only the series of lighted areas beneath the same cast-iron lampposts with their old-fashioned ornaments.

The boy has left again; but instead of turning back, he has continued straight ahead in the same direction. He has covered about a dozen yards and then, suddenly, has begun running. His cape was fluttering behind him. He has continued straight ahead, soon vanishing, appearing again under each street light, disappearing, and again, smaller and smaller, shapeless, blurred by the night and the snow . . .

The soldier is alone, he looks at the door in front of which he is standing. Why has the child shown him this house rather than any other, since he was told only to take him to this street? Which street is this anyway? Is it really the one they were talking about just now? The soldier can no longer remember the name the lame man insisted on so much: it was something like Mallart or Malibar, Malardier, Montoire, Moutardier . . . No, it didn't sound like that.

Against the part of the doorway perpendicular to the wall of the building, on the side receiving a little light from the nearest street light, a small plaque is attached at eye level: some identification concerning the tenant of the building, or at least one of the tenants. There is not enough light for the soldier to read. He puts his hand on it, having stepped onto the stoop, where he balances as well as he can, hampered by its narrowness. The letters are stamped on a cold polished substance, but they are too small and the soldier cannot make out a single word. He notices at this moment that the door is ajar: door, hallway, door, vestibule, door, then finally a lighted room, and a table with an empty glass with a circle of dark-red liquid still at the bottom, and a lame man leaning on his crutch, bend-

ing forward in a precarious balance. No. Door
ajar. Hallway. Staircase. Woman running from
floor to floor up the spiral staircase, her gray
apron billowing about her. Door. And finally a
lighted room: bed, chest, fireplace, table with
a lamp on its left corner, and the lampshade casting a white circle on the ceiling. No. Above the
chest is a print framed in black wood . . . No.
No. No.

The door is not ajar. The soldier moves his
finger across the polished plaque, but his hand
is already numb with cold and he no longer feels
anything at all. Then the door suddenly opens
wide. The hallway is still the same, but this time
it is lighted. There is the naked bulb at the end
of its wire, the civil defense bulletin against the
brown wall near the door, the closed doors to
the right and left, and the staircase at the end
rising in a spiral towards successive walls and
dark corners.

"What do you . . ."

It is another soldier, or rather half a soldier,
for he is wearing a field cap and military jacket,
but black trousers and gray suede shoes. Arms
and legs spread slightly, eyes squinting, mouth
half open, the figure has frozen, startled, threatening, terrified, it retreats down the hallway,
gradually at first, then more and more quickly
but without the feet moving in relation to each

other, the limbs and the whole body remaining rigid as if the whole figure were set on a rail and drawn backward by a thread. No.

While the soldier, having stepped onto the narrow stoop where he balances as well as he can, half leaning against the closed leaf of the door which restricts his movements and compels him to twist his body, his left hand still thrust into the overcoat pocket and his left arm still hugging the package wrapped in brown paper against the hollow of his hip, the other hand raised to the polished plaque attached to the left jamb—while the soldier vainly tries to make out the letters with the tips of his forefinger, middle finger, and ring finger, the door opens so suddenly that he has to grasp the jamb in order not to fall, in order not to be swallowed up by this yawning hallway in the middle of which, just inside the door, stands a man wearing a field cap and military jacket, but civilian trousers and low sport shoes; they probably have rubber soles, for there has been no sound of steps down the hallway. On the collar of the jacket, the two colored diamonds showing the serial number have been removed. In one hand the man is still holding the edge of the door which he has just pivoted on its hinges. His free right hand rises to shoulder height in an uncompleted gesture of welcome, then falls back.

"Come in," he says, "this is the place."

The soldier crosses the threshold, takes three steps down the hallway lit by a naked bulb at the end of a long twisted wire. The soldier stops. The other man has closed the door again. The gust of air has made the lamp move and it now continues to sway at the end of its wire.

The man in the military jacket is again standing motionless in front of the closed door, his arms and legs spread slightly, his hands dangling, in an attitude that is both irresolute and stiff. All the identifying insignia on his clothes have been removed: not only those on the collar, but also the stripes on the sleeves and on the cap, revealing, where they had been, small areas of new material softer and brighter than the faded surrounding areas dirtied by long wear. The difference is so evident that there can be no doubt about the shape of the missing insignia: the infantry diamond, the two parallel, slender, oblique rectangles indicating the rank of corporal; only the colors are missing (bright red, garnet, purple, blue, green, yellow, black . . .) which would furnish precise information as to regiment, duty, etc. The face, in full light now, seems tired, drawn, shrunken, the cheekbones too prominent, the cheeks grayish, the eyes deep in their sockets. The man's shadow is cast against the door to the right, then to the left, then to the right, to the left, to the right, according to the position of the electric bulb swaying at the end of its long wire perpendicular to the direction of the hallway. (The draft from the open door must have moved the lamp longitudinally, but the plane of the oscillations has gradually turned without their amplitude diminishing perceptibly, and the man's foreshortened shadow appears and disappears, now on the right, now on the left, alternately.)

"Are you wounded?" he asks at last.

The soldier shakes his head.

"Sick?"

"No . . . only tired."

"All right, come on up."

But neither one moves, and the man's shadow continues to sway. Then he says: "What do you have in your package?"

The soldier, after a moment's hesitation, looks down toward the brown spotted paper and the distended string.

"Some things."

"What kind of things?"

"My things." He raises his head. The man is still looking at him with the same weary, almost vacant expression.

"Do you have your identification papers?"

"No . . ." The soldier makes a half smile or a fleeting grimace which momentarily distorts his mouth; then his eyebrows rise to indicate his astonishment at this foolish request.

"No, of course not," the other man repeats, and after a few seconds: "All right, come on up."

At this moment the light goes out. Complete darkness replaces the pale, thin face, the dangling hands, and the swaying shadow. At the same time, the ticking, which had been regularly audible without the soldier's being aware of it since the beginning of the scene, has stopped.

And the scene is silent when the light comes on again. The setting is apparently the same: a narrow hallway painted dark brown halfway up the walls, the rest of the walls and the high ceiling being pale beige. But the doors, on the left as on the right, are more numerous. They are, as before, painted dark brown and are of identical dimensions: quite high for their width. The hallway is doubtless longer. The electric bulb is the same: round, quite weak, and hanging at the end of a twisted wire. The light switch, made of white porcelain, is placed just above the stairs at the corner of the wall. The two men are walking slowly, without speaking, one behind the other. The first, the one wearing what was once a corporal's jacket, has just pressed the light switch in passing (was there no switch on the first floor, since they climbed the stairs in darkness?); but the fact that the system is functioning is revealed only by a simple click; the ticking is too faint to be heard over the noise of heavy hobnail boots on the last steps, which the soldier climbs with less difficulty now that he sees clearly. His guide, in front of him, is wearing rubber-soled gray suede shoes; the whisper of his steps is scarcely audible. One behind the other, the two men pass in front of the high, narrow, closed doors on the right and left, one after the other, with their shiny white porcelain knobs that stand out against the dark paint, an egg-shaped object in which the image of the electric bulb makes a luminous speck repeated on the right and the left, in each doorknob, one after the other.

At the very end of the hallway is a last door that resembles the others. The soldier sees the man stop in front of him, his hand on the porcelain knob. When the soldier reaches him, the man quickly opens the door to let the soldier in first, walks in after him and closes the door behind them.

They are standing in a small room, its only illumination a bluish gleam which comes from outside through the six panes of a window that has neither shutters nor curtain. The soldier walks over to the bare panes. He sees the empty street, uniformly white with snow. His hand is resting on the porcelain window fastening which is smooth and cold under his palm. The fastening is not closed, the two leaves of the French window are only pushed shut. They open of their own accord without any effort, by the mere weight of the arm pressing against them. The soldier leans out. It is no longer snowing. The wind has fallen. The night is calm. The soldier leans out a little farther. He sees the sidewalk, much farther down than he expected. Clinging to the sill, he sees beneath him the vertical series of successive windows, and at the bottom the doorway to the building, and the white stoop lighted by the nearby street lamp. The door itself, slightly recessed, is not visible. There are footsteps in the fresh snow, tracks of heavy boots which, coming from the left along the buildings, lead to the doorway and end there just beneath his eyes. A vague mass moves in the doorway. It looks like a man in a cloak or a military overcoat. He has stepped onto the stoop and his body is pressed against the door. But the part of his body outside the doorway clearly reveals a shoulder with a buttoned tab, a bent arm holding under the elbow a rectangular package the size of a shoe box.

"You don't look as if you were feeling very well," the man says as he comes toward him. The soldier has sat down on the first chair his hand encountered behind him. The man, who had gone to look for something at the back of the room, has returned holding in his arms a rather large bundle difficult to identify in this lunar half light: cloth . . .

"You don't look as if you were feeling very well."

"I don't know . . . ," the soldier answers passing his hand across his face, "no . . . it's nothing." His other hand has remained in his overcoat pocket. He readjusts the package in the crook of his elbow. He sees the vertical series of successive windows, each one with a white line at the bottom of the snowy window recess, the vertical series of parallel rungs descending to the stoop—like a falling stone. He stands up and walks mechanically behind the man who is heading for the door. He is holding bedclothes under his arm. In the hallway, the light has gone out again.

They are standing in a long room lighted with blue electric bulbs. There are beds lined up on each side against both walls: on the left, a bare partition and on the right a series of equidistant windows whose six panes are covered with paper. The windows seem to be level with the wall, without the slightest inside recess; only their dark color distinguishes them; since the wall around them and the paper neatly covering each

pane are of the same pale shade, in this blue
light they look like imitation windows: a heavily
drawn rectangle divided into six equal squares
by thinner lines: a vertical central axis and two
horizontals which cut it into thirds. Coming from
the total darkness of the hallway, the soldier advances without difficulty between the two neat
rows of metal beds; this dim lighting is enough
for him to distinguish clearly the outline of
things.

Men are lying on almost all the beds, covered with dark blankets. The man with the unsewn chevrons has led the soldier to the middle
of the row on the side of the wall without windows, and has indicated an empty mattress by
setting the bedclothes down on it; then he has
left again without further explanations, and he
has closed the door behind him.

The folded bedclothes form two dark rectangles against the lighter background of the
mattress, two rectangles which overlap at one
corner. The beds to the right and left are both
occupied: two bodies lying on their backs,
wrapped in their blankets; the heads are supported by bolsters of the same light shade as
the mattresses; the man on the right has also put
his hands under his neck, the folded elbows
pointing diagonally on each side. The man is
not sleeping: his eyes are wide open. The man on

the left, whose arms are hidden alongside his body, is also not sleeping. Others farther away, lying on their sides, have their bodies slightly raised on one elbow. One man is even half sitting up: in the dim light he stares at the newcomer who is standing in front of his bed, one hand resting its fingertips on the horizontal iron bar which comprises its foot, the other in the overcoat pocket, a shoe box under the arm. Everyone is perfectly motionless and silent. Doubtless they are not sleepy: it is still too early; and the lack of adequate light prevents them from doing anything but lying here, eyes wide open, staring at the motionless newcomer with his shoe box or at the imitation windows in front of them, or at the bare wall, or the ceiling, or into space.

The soldier finally approaches the head of the bed while he takes in his right hand the package he was holding under his left arm. And again he stands perfectly still. This room, as he now notices, differs in one important detail from the dormitories of a military barracks: there is no kit shelf running along the wall over the beds. The soldier stands with his box in his hands, wondering where he can put it for the night, hesitating to let it out of his sight or to draw more attention to it. After considerable indecision, he pulls the bolster away from the painted iron grill that forms the head of the bed, sets the box down on the end of the mattress, and pushes the bolster back against it in order to secure it firmly. He decides that this way, when his head is on the bolster, any attempt to take the box will awaken him no matter how heavily he is sleeping. Then, sitting on the bed and leaning forward, he slowly begins removing his leggings, coiling up the strip of material as he unwraps it from around his leg.

"You don't even know how to wrap your leggings." At the foot of the lamppost, on the edge of the sidewalk, the boy stares at the soldier's ankles. Then, raising his eyes, he examines his entire outfit from his feet to his head, his gaze finally coming to rest on the hollow cheeks black with their growth of beard: "Where did you sleep last night?"

The soldier replies with a vague gesture. Still bending forward, he unties one shoe lace. The child begins to move away slowly, disappearing toward the rear of the scene but without turning around, without moving, his serious eyes still staring at the soldier beneath the navy blue beret pulled down on each side over his ears, holding the edges of his cape together from the inside, while his whole body seems to glide backwards across the snow-covered sidewalk along the flat housefronts, passing the ground floor windows one after the other: four identical windows followed by a door only slightly larger, then four more windows, a door, a window, a window, a window, a window, a door, a window, a window, faster and faster as he moves farther away, becoming smaller and smaller, vaguer and vaguer, fainter and fainter in the twilight, suddenly swallowed up toward the horizon and then disappearing in the wink of an eye, like a falling stone.

The soldier is lying on his mattress fully dressed, having merely taken off his heavy boots which he has put under the bed beside his leggings. He has wrapped himself up in the two blankets, over the overcoat which he has simply unbuttoned at the collar, too tired to make one more gesture. Besides, the room is not heated save by the bodies of the men lying there. There is no large square porcelain stove near the rear door at the end of the counter with its pipe bent at right angles and joining the wall above the shelves full of bottles. But the main thing is to be sheltered from the falling snow and the wind.

His eyes wide open, the soldier continues to stare into the darkness in front of him, a few yards in front of him, where the child stands, motionless and rigid too, his arms at his sides. But it is as if the soldier did not see the child— neither the child nor anything else.

He has long since emptied his glass. He does

not seem to be planning to leave. Yet around him, the room has been emptied of its last customers, and the bartender has gone out through the rear door after having turned out most of the lamps.

"You can't sleep here, you know."

Behind the table and the empty glass, behind the child, behind the large window with its pleated curtain which covers it halfway up, its three spheres arranged in a triangle and its inscription in reverse, the white flakes are still falling just as slowly, their descent vertical and regular. It is doubtless this continuous, uniform, immutable movement that the soldier is staring at, motionless at his table between his two companions. The child sitting on the floor in the foreground is also looking in this direction, although without raising his head he cannot see the bare panes above the pleated curtain. As for the other people, they do not seem to be concerned with what is happening over here: the group of seated drinkers talking heatedly and gesticulating, the crowd at the rear moving toward the left of the picture, where the overloaded coat racks are, the group standing at the right facing the wall, reading the bulletin which has been tacked there, and the bartender behind his bar, leaning forward toward the six men in middle-class clothes forming a small circle with emphatic postures, caught motionless like all the others in the middle of gestures which this arbitrary pause has deprived of any naturalness, like people at a party whom a photographer has tried to catch in candid movement, but whom technical necessities have kept too long in one position: "Don't move now! . . ." An arm remains half raised, a mouth gapes, a head is tipped back; but tension has replaced movement, the features are contorted, the limbs stiffened, the smile has become a grimace, the impulse has lost its intention and its meaning. There no longer remains, in their place, anything but excess, and strangeness, and death.

The six men in long frock coats who are standing in front of the bar, under the eye of the bartender whose thickset body, leaning toward them, is supported on his hands that grip the inner edge of the bar, on top of which are set the six glasses, still full, belonging to the customers momentarily distracted from their thirst by a discussion doubtless full of excitement and noise—a fist raised in anger, a head thrown back to shout the swearwords which the mouth shapes with violence, and the other men in the group approving, punctuating the remark with other solemn gestures, all talking or exclaiming at the same time—the six characters grouped in the left foreground are the ones who first catch the eye.

But the most noticeable man of the group is perhaps not the short fat man declaiming in the center, nor the four others around him (two seen full face, one in profile, one from behind) who are echoing his words, but the last man, situated behind them and slightly to one side, almost a head taller than his companions. His dress is apparently similar, as far as can be judged, since his body is almost completely hidden by his neighbors, except for the open collar above a wide white cravat and a well-fitted shoulder, and the opposite arm, which reappears behind one of the heads, stretched out to rest forearm and hand on the rounded edge of the counter in front of a glass shaped like a truncated cone mounted on a circular foot.

This last man seems uninterested in what his friends are saying and doing right in front of him. He is staring over the seated drinkers at the one female figure in the entire scene: a slender waitress standing in the middle of the room, carrying a tray with only one bottle on it among the benches, the tables, the chairs, and the bodies of the workers facing in different directions. She is wearing a simple long-sleeved dress with a full-pleated skirt gathered at the waist. She has thick black hair in a bun and a regular face with sharp but delicate features. Her movements give the impression of a certain grace. It is difficult to know which way she is going because of the pronounced torsion of her waist and her entire body; her profile does not indicate the same direction as her hips, so that she seems to be glancing at all the tables around the room to see if anyone is calling for her, while she raises the tray over her head in both hands. The tray, moreover, is tilting alarmingly, as is the liter bottle balanced on top of it. Instead of keeping her eye on this precarious burden, the woman is looking in the opposite direction, her head turned more than ninety degrees away from the tray toward the right side of the scene and the round table where the three soldiers are sitting.

It is not certain that she is looking only at them: other customers are also within her field of vision beyond this particular table, some civilians at another table, less apparent because drawn in vaguer outline, but still just as noticeable to the waitress herself. And in fact one of the latter seems to be holding up a hand to attract her attention.

But the look which the eye (seen in profile) of the young woman with black hair would direct toward this extended arm in the background would in any case cross the raised face of the soldier who is sitting facing her, a companion on either side (whose faces are not visible in the picture), an impassive face with features lined by fatigue, contrasting by its calm with the contortions and grimaces prevalent everywhere else. His hands, similarly, are lying flat on the table which is covered with a red-and-white checked oilcloth, where glasses, set down several times, have left a number of circular marks, some incomplete, some dry, some quite distinct, others completely obliterated by the sliding of a glass, or by an overcoat sleeve, or by a wipe of a rag.

And now the woman is sitting on a chair facing the soldier on the other side of the table with its red-and-white oilcloth which hangs in stiff folds over the edges. While the soldier is slowly chewing the bread which she has gone to get for him, along with the glass and the bottle, he stares at the half-closed door which reveals a child's figure in its opening. The young woman with black hair and pale eyes has just asked her questions about the regiment to which her visitor belongs—to which at least the latter's uniform and military insignia belong.

In the ensuing silence, when the soldier has raised his eyes to his hostess, the latter's head shifts slightly with a counter-clockwise movement toward the portrait fastened to the wall over the chest. It is a full length photograph of her husband, taken the morning he left for the front during the first days of the offensive, during the period when everyone behind the lines was convinced of an easy and rapid victory. Since then she has had no word from him. All she knows is that the unit he was fighting in was in the Reichenfels area at the time of the enemy breakthrough.

The soldier asks her which unit this was. Although her answer is not very exact, and although she has no idea of army organization, it seems that the position the woman gives is mistaken: the battalion she is talking about was never under fire, it was surrounded and disarmed much farther west. However, the soldier has no desire to begin a discussion on this subject, particularly since the young woman might feel he had insulting intentions concerning her husband's military career. He therefore confines himself to making a general remark: there were many less troops in Reichenfels than was subsequently claimed.

"Then you think he's a prisoner?"

"Yes," he says, "probably," which does not commit him to much, for unless he is dead the husband will soon be a prisoner in any case.

It is at this moment that the lame man has come into the room, through the half-open door to the next room, advancing without any evident awkwardness among the various obstacles, maneuvering his wooden crutch with agility. And the boy has soon reappeared at the other door.

It is this boy who afterwards leads the soldier through the empty streets as night falls, along the housefronts with their unlighted windows. Yet there are still inhabitants in the city; a large part of the civilian population must not have left it when there was still time. Does no one, then, dare turn on a light in rooms overlooking the street? Why do these people still obey the outdated civil defense instructions? Probably out of habit; or else because there is no administration to repeal the old regulations which of course would no longer apply. Besides, the city lighting system is functioning just as in peacetime; there are even street lights that have remained on all day long.

But the windows succeeding each other along the flat housefronts, on the ground floor as on every floor of the high uniform houses, do not reveal the least gleam of light, yet no shutter nor curtain has been drawn in front of or behind the panes, which are as black and bare as if all these apartments were uninhabited, gleaming only occasionally, at certain fleeting angles, with the brief reflection of a street light.

The boy seems to be going faster and faster, and the soldier, too exhausted, no longer manages to follow him. The slender figure, wrapped in its black cape, beneath which appear the two narrow black trouser legs, gets farther and farther ahead. The soldier is constantly afraid he has lost it. Then he catches a glimpse of it far ahead, much farther than he expected, suddenly illuminated as it passes under a street light, then immediately disappearing in the darkness again, invisible once more.

Hence the child may at any moment turn into a side street without being seen, for the route he has taken from the start is far from being straight. Luckily the fresh snow on the sidewalk shows his footprints, the only ones on the entire smooth surface between the housefronts and the parallel edge of the gutter, clear tracks despite the boy's rapidity, shallowly printed in the thin layer of new snow which has just fallen on the paths trampled hard during the day, footprints of chevroned rubber soles with a cross inscribed in a circle on the heel.

Now the tracks stop suddenly in front of a door just like the others, but not completely closed. The stoop is very narrow and can be crossed in one stride without setting foot on it. The light at the other end of the hallway is on; the ticking sounds like an alarm clock. At the far end of the hallway is a rather narrow staircase rising in short flights, separated by small square landings, turning at right angles. The floor landings, despite the many doors which open off them, are scarcely any larger. At the top is the closed room where the gray film of dust gradually settles on the table and on the small objects on top of it, on the mantelpiece, on the marble top of the chest, on the day bed, on the waxed floor where the felt slippers . . .

The tracks continue, regular and straight, across the fresh snow. They continue for hours, a right foot, a left foot, a right foot, for hours. And the soldier is still walking, mechanically, numb with cold and fatigue, mechanically setting one foot in front of the other without even being sure he is making any progress, for the same regular footprints are always there in the same places under his own feet. Since the spacing of the chevroned soles corresponds to his own stride (that of a man at the end of his strength), he has naturally begun putting his feet in the footprints already made. His boot is a little larger, but this is scarcely noticeable in the snow. Suddenly he has the feeling he has already been here, ahead of himself.

But the snow was still falling, at this moment, in close flakes, and no sooner were the guide's footprints made than they immediately began to lose their clarity and quickly filled up, becoming more and more unrecognizable as the distance increased between him and the soldier, their mere presence soon becoming a matter of doubt, a scarcely noticeable depression in the uniformity of the snow's surface, finally disappearing altogether for several yards . . .

The soldier thinks he has definitely lost the track when he sees the boy waiting for him a few feet away, under a street light, huddled in his black cape already white with snow.

"Here it is," he says, pointing to a door just like the others.

Then there is the electric bulb swaying at the end of its long wire and the man's shadow swaying across the closed door like a slow metronome.

During the night the soldier awakens with a start. The blue bulbs are still on, hanging from the ceiling, a row of three down the center of the room. In a single movement the soldier has thrown back his covers and sat up on the edge of his bed, his feet on the floor. He was dreaming that the alarm signal had sounded. He was in a winding trench whose top reached as high as his forehead; in his hand he was holding some kind of grenade, elongated in shape, with a delayed-action explosion device which he had just set going. Without a second to lose he had to throw it out of the trench. He heard it ticking steadily like an alarm clock. But he stood there with the grenade in his hand, his arm extended as if to throw it, inexplicably paralyzed, increasingly rigid, less and less able to move even a finger as the moment of the explosion approached. He must have shouted in his sleep to escape the nightmare.

Yet the other sleepers seem perfectly calm. Probably he has not really cried out. Looking more carefully, he discovers that his neighbor's eyes are wide open: both hands under his neck, he continues to stare straight ahead into the darkness.

Half intending to find some water to drink, half to look as if he knew what he were doing, the soldier stands up and, without putting on his shoes in order to avoid making noise, leaves the row of beds and heads for the door through which he first came. He is thirsty. Not only his throat feels dry, but his whole body is burning despite the cold. He reaches the door and tries to turn the handle, but the lock resists. He dare not shake it too hard for fear of waking everyone. Besides, the door seems to be locked.

Having turned around, panic-stricken, he realizes that the windows, the imitation windows drawn in black on the wall, are now on his left although they were on his right when he came into this room the first time. He then notices a second, identical door at the other end of the long passage between the two rows of beds. Realizing that he must have turned the wrong way, he crosses the entire length of the room between the two rows of prone bodies. All the eyes are wide open and watch him pass, in complete silence.

As a matter of fact, the other door opens easily. The latrines are located at the other end of the hall. The soldier noticed this as he came upstairs, before lying down. Intending to shift the package wrapped in brown paper under his arm, he suddenly remembers having left it unguarded beneath the bolster. He immediately closes the door again and quickly returns to his bed. At first glance he sees that the bolster is now lying flat against the vertical iron bars; he approaches and discovers that the box is no longer there; he turns the bolster over as if it were necessary to convince himself further of the fact, turns the bolster over twice more; finally he straightens up, no longer knowing what to do, but there are no longer blankets on the mattress either. And three beds farther along the soldier recognizes some blankets bundled into a ball on an empty mattress. He has simply gone to the wrong bed.

On his bed, everything is where it was:

blankets, bolster, and package. And, under the bed, the boots and the coiled-up leggings are also there. The soldier lies down again without having had anything to drink. Despite his burning throat, he no longer has the strength to make another attempt, to walk through the labyrinth of unlighted hallways until he reaches this infinitely distant and problematical water. His passages through the dormitory have occurred very quickly, in the last restlessness of a feverish awakening. He now feels incapable of taking another step. Moreover, he could not go out carrying his big box without awakening or reinforcing futile suspicions; his recent behavior has made him only too noticeable already. He scarcely takes the time to wrap his feet and legs in one of the blankets before stretching out again, spreading the second blanket over his whole body as well as he can. And once more he is walking in the snow through the empty streets along the high, flat housefronts which succeed each other indefinitely, without variation. His route is punctuated by black lampposts with stylized ornaments of old-fashioned elegance, their electric bulbs shining with a yellow luster in the leaden daylight.

The soldier walks as fast as he can without running, as though he feared someone might be pursuing him and that all the same too evident a flight might arouse the suspicion of passers-by. But no figure appears as far as the eye can see toward the gray end of the straight street, and each time the soldier turns around to look back, continuing straight ahead without slowing down, he can see that no pursuer threatens to catch up with him: the white sidewalk stretches behind him as empty as in the other direction, with only the line of footprints made by his hobnail boots, slightly distorted each time the soldier has turned around.

He was waiting on a street corner near a lamppost. He was looking at the corner of the house opposite him on the other side of the street. He had already been looking at it for some time when he noticed that there were some people in a room on the third floor. This was a rather large room with no visible furniture and two windows; the figures came and went from one window to the other, but without coming near the panes, which had no curtains. The soldier particularly noticed their pale faces in the room's half-darkness. The room must have had dark walls to make these faces stand out so clearly. The people seemed to be talking to each other, consulting each other; they made gestures, as the relative whiteness of their hands indicated. They were looking at something in the street, and the subject of their discussion seemed of some importance. Suddenly the soldier realized that this could only be himself. There was nothing else outside those windows on the sidewalk or in the street. To disguise his intentions the soldier began examining his surroundings, staring at the horizon first in one direction, then the other. Not exactly to disguise his intentions, but to show that he was expecting someone and was not concerned with the house in front of which he merely happened to be standing.

When he again glanced furtively toward the third floor windows, the pale faces had come noticeably closer to the bare panes. One of the figures was obviously pointing at him, hand outstretched; the other faces were grouped around the first at various levels, as if some of their possessors were standing, some crouching, others on tiptoe or even on chairs; the other window was empty.

"They think I'm a spy," the soldier decided. Preferring not to have to refute this accusation, which risked being formulated in a more immediate way, he pretended to consult a non-existent watch on his wrist and walked off without further thought down the next cross street.

After about ten steps he decided his behavior was foolish: it merely confirmed the suspicions of his observers, who would lose no time following him. Instinctively he began to walk faster. Imagining he heard behind him the sound of a window being flung open, he even had difficulty keeping himself from running.

The soldier turns around once more to look behind him: there is still no one. But as he turns back in the direction he is walking, he now sees the boy who seems to be waiting for him as he passes, half hidden behind the corner of a house at the next crossroad.

This time the soldier stops short. The door of the apartment house on his left is half-open, revealing a dark hallway. Farther on, at the crossroads, the child has stepped back a little so that he is entirely concealed by the stone corner of the building. The soldier suddenly turns into the door and finds himself in the hallway. At the far end, without losing a minute, he begins climbing the short flights of the narrow staircase which turns at right angles, each flight separated from the next by a small square landing.

On the top floor, there is the room sealed behind its thick curtains. The shoe box wrapped in brown paper is lying on the chest, the dagger-bayonet on the marble mantlepiece. The dust has already covered the heavy double-edged blade with a thin layer which dims the metal's luster under the shaded light from the lamp on the table. The shadow of the fly on the ceiling continues its circuit.

To the right of the large luminous circle whose circumference it regularly follows, there is, at the corner of the ceiling, a slender black line about an inch long and scarcely noticeable: a crack in the plaster, or a spider web covered with dust, or some trace of a bump or scratch. This imperfection in the white surface, moreover, is not equally visible from every point in the room. It is particularly apparent to an observer near the base of the wall to the right, at the other end of the room, looking up along what is virtually the diagonal of this wall, as is normal for someone lying on the bed, his head resting on the bolster.

The soldier is lying on his bed. It is probably the cold which has awakened him. He is on his back, in the same position he was in when he first opened his eyes; he has not moved since. In front of him the windows are wide open. On the other side of the street there are other windows identical to these. In the room all the men are still lying down. Most of them look as if they are sleeping. Nor does he know what time it is now. His immediate neighbors, to the right and left, are wrapped as closely as possible in their blankets; one of them, who has turned toward him, has even covered part of his face, leaving only his nose sticking out, while a flap of material pulled over his head covers his eyes as well. Although it is difficult to tell what kind of clothes the sleepers are wearing, it appears that none of them has undressed for the night, for there are no clothes to be seen hanging somewhere or folded up or thrown down at random. Moreover, there are no closets or shelves or cupboards of any kind, and only the bed ends could be used to hang coats, jackets, and trousers on; but these bed ends, made of metal rods painted white, are all as unencumbered at the foot as at the head. Without moving his body, the soldier pats his bolster behind him in order to make sure his box is still there.

He must get up now. If he does not succeed in giving this package to its intended recipient, he at least has the chance of getting rid of it while there is still time. Tomorrow, tonight, or even in a few hours, it will be too late. In any case, he has no reason to stay here doing nothing; a prolonged stay in this psuedo-barracks, or infirmary, or hospitalization center, can only make new complications for him, and he may thereby be compromising his last chances of success.

The soldier tries to raise himself on his elbows. His entire body is paralyzed. Having
slipped only a few inches on his back toward the
head of the bed, he lets himself fall back, his
shoulders leaning against the vertical iron rods
supporting the upper, thicker bar against which
his head rests. The box, luckily, is in no danger
of being crushed. The soldier turns his face to
the right, where there is a door through which
he should be leaving.

Next to the man whose face is hooded in a
flap of the coarse brown blanket, the sleeper
beyond has one arm outside his blankets, an
arm wearing the khaki sleeve of a military jacket.
The reddish hand hangs over the edge of the
mattress. Farther along, other bodies are lying
stretched out or curled up. Several have kept
their field caps on.

At the end of the room, the door has opened
noiselessly and two men have come in, one behind the other. The first is a civilian, wearing
hunting clothes: heavy leather boots, narrow
riding breeches, a thick duffle-coat, and a long
muffler around his neck. He has kept on a faded
felt hat, shapeless with age and wear; his entire
outfit is worn, tattered, and even rather dirty.
The second man is the one from the evening before, wearing his jacket and corporal's cap with
its unsewn stripes. Without stopping at the first

beds, without even glancing at them in passing,
they have advanced down the central space to
one of the sleepers in the opposite row under
the second window. Stopping at the foot of the
bed, the two men speak together in low voices.
Then the civilian in the felt hat approaches the
pillow and touches the body near the shoulder.
At once the body, wrapped in blankets, sits up
and a pale face appears, the eyes deep in their
sockets, the hollow cheeks blackened by several days' growth of beard. Startled out of his
sleep, the man takes some time to get his bear-
ings, while the two others stand motionless beside him. He passes one hand over his eyes,
across his forehead, and through his short, grayish hair. Then he begins to lean back and suddenly collapses on his mattress.

The civilian must be some kind of doctor or
hospital attendant, for he then carefully grasps
the man's wrist and holds it between his fingers
for some time, as if he were taking the man's
pulse, although without consulting any watch.
He then lays the inert arm alongside the prone
body. He exchanges a few more words with the
man accompanying him; after which the two
of them cross the width of the room diagonally
to reach the patient whose red hand sticks out
of the blankets and hangs over the edge of the
mattress. Leaning forward in order not to move

the sleeper's hand, the attendant grasps it as he did the one before, without in this case producing the slightest reaction. The examination lasts a little longer this time, and afterwards the two men have a longer conversation in low voices. Finally they move away from the bed without having awakened the patient.

The attendant now glances around the rest of the room; he stops at the newcomer, who, unlike his comrades, is half sitting up on his bed. The corporal with the unsewn stripes gestures with his chin to indicate him and says something like: "arrived last night." They come closer. The corporal remains at the foot of the bed. The other man comes to the pillow. The soldier mechanically holds out his wrist, which the attendant grasps firmly without asking any questions. After a few seconds he declares in a low voice, as if he were talking to himself: "You have fever."

"It's nothing much," the soldier says, but his own voice, weak and hoarse, surprises him.

"A high fever," the other man repeats, letting go of his hand.

The hand falls back, inert, on the mattress. The corporal has taken a black notebook and a short pencil out of his pocket and writes some information which the soldier has no difficulty making out: the day and hour of his arrival, the serial number on his overcoat collar, this number 12,345 which has never been his.

"Has it been long?" asks the attendant in the felt hat.

"Long since I've been here?"

"No, since you've had fever."

"I don't know," the soldier says.

The man turns back to his colleague and they step toward the windows for a short discussion which the soldier cannot hear, nor can he read the words on their lips, for he does not see their faces. But the attendant comes back toward him; he leans over and with both hands at once feels each side of his chest through the various layers of clothing:

"Does it hurt when I press?"

"No . . . not any more."

"You've been sleeping like this?"

"What do you mean like this?"

"With a wet coat."

The soldier now pats the stiff, rough material that is still somewhat damp. He says: "It must be the snow . . ."

His words are so faint that they disintegrate before he has spoken them; afterwards he even doubts whether he has actually pronounced them at all.

The attendant now addresses his colleague: "It would be better to change him."

"I'll go see if I have something," the other man says, and he immediately walks to the door, his steps soundless.

Remaining alone, the attendant buttons his dun-colored canvas duffle-coat that is faded and spotted down the front, forcing the three braided-leather buttons into their loops; all three are damaged, the bottom one split by a large scratch halfway through its width, leaving a strip of leather that protrudes about a quarter of an inch. The attendant has put his hands in his shapeless side pockets. He stares at the soldier for a moment and asks:

"Aren't you cold?"

"No . . . Yes . . . A little."

"We can close this now," the man says, and without waiting for his interlocutor's agreement, he moves toward the left end of the dormitory to close the last window. Then he moves along the wall toward the right, slipping between the wall and the iron rods that form the heads of the beds, and continues the operation, coming closer and closer, pulling in the French windows and closing the fastenings which he is obliged to force, making several attempts. As he advances, the daylight wanes in the large room, the darkness increasing from the left and gradually thickening.

There are five windows. Each has two leaves

with three square panes in it. But these panes are visible only when the window is open, for the inner side is covered with dark, translucent paper pasted neatly over the entire surface of the pane. When the man is through, the entire room is plunged into half-darkness, the five rectangular openings are replaced by five series of six purplish, vaguely luminous panes through which filters a light like those of the blue night lamps, all the more inadequate since it succeeds the bright daylight without any transition. The man in the duffle-coat and the felt hat at the right end of the room is only a black silhouette, motionless against the lighter wall, near the outside door.

The soldier supposes that the visitor is about to leave the room, but instead he turns toward his bed:

"There," he says, "now you won't be so cold." And, after a silence: "They'll bring you other clothes. But you have to stay in bed."

He stops talking again; then he resumes: "The doctor will come soon, maybe this afternoon, or later this morning, or tonight . . ." At times he speaks so low that the soldier has trouble hearing him.

"Meanwhile," he continues, "you'll take the pills they give you . . . You mustn't . . ." The end of his sentence is inaudible. He has taken a pair of heavy fur-lined gloves out of his pocket and slowly pulls them on, still adjusting them as he moves away. After several yards all that can be seen of him is a vague shadow; and even before he has reached the door he disappears altogether. Only his heavy boots can be heard continuing on their way with slow steps.

There is no longer light enough to make out the positions of the sleepers. The soldier imagines that this will make it easier for him to leave the dormitory without being seen. He will get a drink as he leaves, from the latrines down the hall.

He makes another effort to sit up and this time succeeds. But he is still leaning against the metal bar behind him. In order to make his position more comfortable he raises the bolster behind him and puts it on top of the box. Then he leans to the right, his hand reaching toward the floor for his boots. At this moment he notices a black silhouette in front of him whose head and bust are outlined against the luminous panes of mauve paper. He recognizes his host of the night before, the corporal without stripes, with his pointed field cap. The soldier's right hand returns to its place on the mattress.

The man puts something that looks like a heavy overcoat across the iron crosspiece at the foot of the bed. Then he steps forward between the two beds and hands the soldier a glass three-quarters full of a colorless liquid.

"Drink this," he says, "it's water. There are pills in the bottom. Afterwards you'll have coffee along with the others."

The soldier seizes the glass and drinks greedily, but the half-dissolved pills which he swallows with the last mouthful stick in his throat and there is no more water to help him get them down. There is a kind of bitter granular deposit which stays in his throat and makes him feel as though it were stripped raw. He feels even thirstier than before.

The man has taken back the empty glass. He observes the whitish streaks which have remained on the sides. Finally he goes away after pointing at the foot of the bed: "I've brought you another overcoat," he says, "put it on before you lie down again."

An indeterminable period after the silent shadow has vanished, the soldier decides to get up. He pivots his legs carefully and sits on the edge of the bed, his knees bent, his feet resting on the floor. Letting his body settle a little, he waits for a long time, at least so it seems to him.

Before going any further he throws off his blankets, which now form a pile on the mattress. Then, leaning down, he gropes about for his boots; having found them under his fingers, he pulls them on, one after the other, and begins lacing them up. Mechanically he unrolls his leggings and wraps them around his calves.

But he has considerable difficulty standing up, as if the weight and burden of his body had become those of a diving suit. Then he begins walking without too much difficulty. Trying to avoid making loud noises with his hobnail boots on the floor, he leaves the row of beds, and without hesitating more than a few seconds, turns right toward the door. He immediately changes his mind and turns back to inspect the overcoat left by the corporal. It is virtually the same as his own, perhaps less worn. The distinctive mark of the regiment—a felt diamond bearing the serial number—has been unsewn from the collar tab on each side.

The soldier lays the garment across the end of the bed and examines it in the darkness, his mind a blank, supporting himself with one hand on the horizontal iron bar. At the other end of the bed he sees the box, still under the bolster. He moves to the head of the bed, rolls back the bolster, picks up the box, puts it under his left arm. At its touch, he feels the dampness of the wool cloth. He puts both hands in his pockets. The lining is wet and cold.

Coming back to the dry overcoat, in the same spot as before, he waits for another moment before leaving. If he exchanges coats, he will not have to unsew the red felt diamonds on his collar. He takes his hands out of his pockets, puts the box down on the bed, slowly unbuttons the overcoat he is wearing. But at first he cannot extricate his arms from the sleeves, because the joints of his shoulders have become so stiff. When he is finally rid of the wet coat, he lets himself rest a minute before continuing the operation. The two coats are now beside each other across the metal bar. In any case, he must put one of them back on. He picks up the new one and slips into the sleeves quite easily, buttons up the four buttons, picks up the box again, puts it back under his left arm, thrusts his hands into the pockets.

This time he has not forgotten anything. He walks carefully toward the door. At the bottom of his right pocket, his hand encounters a round, hard, smooth, cold object the size of a large marble.

In the lighted hallway he passes the corporal who stops to watch him go by, seemingly on the point of speaking when the soldier goes into the latrine—normal behavior, after all; the corporal may think he has taken his package with him because it contains toilet articles.

When he comes out again, having drunk a great deal of cold water from the tap, the corporal

is no longer there. The soldier continues down
the hall to the stairway; he begins to walk down,
holding onto the railing with his right hand.
Although he watches his movements carefully,
the stiffness of his knees forces him to advance
both heavily and mechanically, and the impact
of his heavy boots echoes against the wooden
steps, one after the other. At each landing the
soldier stops; but as soon as he begins going
down again, the noise of his hobnail boots on
the steps resumes—regular, heavy, isolated, echoing through the house, as in an abandoned
building.

At the foot of the staircase, in front of the
last step of the last flight, the lame man is leaning on his wooden crutch. The crutch is thrust
forward against the steps; the whole body leans
forward in what seems a precarious balance; the
face is raised, frozen in a forced smile of welcome.

"How are you," he says. "Slept well?"

The soldier too is motionless now. His package under one arm, the other hand on the railing. He is standing at the edge of the first landing between flights, seven or eight steps higher
than his interlocutor. He answers: "I'm all right,"
in a hesitant tone of voice.

In his present position, the lame man is
standing in his way. The soldier would have to

shove him aside in order to step off the stairs and reach the door to the street. The soldier wonders if this is the same person as the man he met in the apartment of the woman with pale eyes. The man, as a matter of fact, who told him of the existence of this psuedo-barracks for invalids. If it's not the same man, why should he speak to the soldier as if he knew him? If it is the same man, how did he get here on his crutch through the snow-covered streets? And why?

"Is the lieutenant up there?"

"The lieutenant?"

"Yes, the lieutenant! Is he up there?"

The soldier hesitates to answer. He moves closer to the railing in order to lean on it, but he does not want to show how tired he is, stands as straight as possible, and speaks as clearly as he can: "Which lieutenant?"

"The one in charge of this place. You know!"

The soldier realizes that he should at least pretend to know what the man is talking about: "Yes," he says, "he's up there."

He wonders how the lame man will manage to climb the stairs with his crutch, which he generally uses so skillfully. Perhaps he has stopped at the bottom of the stairs because it is impossible for him to climb them. In any case, he is not making the slightest gesture now, merely staring at the soldier, neither stepping back to let him pass nor advancing to meet him.

"I see you've unsewn your number."

The smile on the raised face has grown broader, twisting the mouth and the whole side of the face.

"That was a good idea," the man continues, "in any case it's safer."

To cut short the conversation, the soldier decides to step forward. He comes down one step, but the lame man has not moved an inch, so that the soldier's second foot now stops beside the first, instead of moving down to the next step.

"Where are you going now?" the lame man asks.

The soldier shrugs evasively: "I have things to do."

"And what have you got in your box?" the lame man asks.

Starting down the stairs without stopping this time, the soldier grumbles an irritated answer: "Nothing much." Standing opposite the man, he suddenly flattens himself against the railing. Nimbly the lame man shifts his crutch and moves toward the wall. The soldier passes in front of him and continues down the hallway. He has no need to turn around to know that the lame man is staring after him, leaning forward on his crutch.

The door to the street is not locked. As he is turning the handle the soldier hears the bantering, vaguely threatening voice behind him: "You seem to be in a hurry this morning." He goes out the door and closes it behind him. On the stamped metal plaque fastened to the jamb he reads: "Headquarters, Military Stores of the North and Northwest Regions."

It is so cold in the street that the soldier is shocked. Yet he feels that the cold is doing him good. But he would like to sit down. He must content himself with leaning against the stone wall, setting his feet on the strip of fresh snow between the housefronts and the trampled, yellowish path. In his overcoat pocket his right hand again comes in contact with the large, smooth marble.

It is an ordinary glass marble about an inch in diameter. Its entire surface is completely regular and highly polished. The interior is colorless and transparent except for a central opaque nucleus the size of a pea. This nucleus is black and round. From whatever angle the marble is examined, the nucleus appears as a black disc a fraction of an inch across. Around it the mass of limpid glass reveals only unrecognizable fragments of the red-and-white pattern of which it occupies a circular fraction. Beyond this circle extends on all sides the checkerboard pattern of the oilcloth covering the table. But in the surface of the marble is also reflected, pale and distorted and greatly reduced in scale, the furnishings of the café.

The child rolls the marble gently across the red-and-white checked oilcloth, not pushing it hard enough to make it move beyond the edges of the rectangular surface. It crosses the latter diagonally, follows the long side, returns to its point of departure. Then the child picks it up, stares at it a long time, turning it round and round. Then his large serious eyes shift to the soldier: "What's inside it?" he says, in his voice which is too low to be a boy's.

"I don't know. Glass too, probably."

"It's black."

"Yes, it's black glass."

The child examines the marble again and asks: "Why?" And when the soldier does not answer he repeats: "Why is it inside?"

"I don't know," the soldier says, then after a few seconds: "To look pretty probably."

"But it's not pretty," the child says.

He has lost almost all his mistrust now, and although his voice still has its grave, almost adult timbre, he speaks with a childish simplicity, sometimes even with a naïve abandon. He is still wearing his black cape over his shoulders, but he has taken off his beret, revealing his short blond hair parted on the right.

This boy is the one from the café, apparently, who is not the same as the one who took the soldier (or who will take him, afterwards) to the barracks—from which, as a matter of fact, he has brought back the marble. In any case, it is this boy who has brought the soldier into the café run by the large, thickset, taciturn man, where he has drunk a glass of red wine and eaten two slices of stale bread. He felt stronger after this snack, and to thank the child he has given him the glass marble that was in his over-coat pocket.

"Are you really giving it to me?"

"Yes, I told you so."

"Where does it come from?"

"From my pocket."

"And before that?"

"Before that? I don't know about before that," the soldier says.

The child glances at him inquisitively, and probably incredulously. He immediately be-comes somewhat more reserved again and his voice is much colder when he remarks, his eyes fixed on the overcoat collar:

"You've unsewn your number."

The soldier tries to make a joke of the matter. "It's no use any more, you know."

The child does not smile. He does not look as if the explanation were satisfactory.

"But I know it," he says. "It was 12,345."

The soldier does not answer. The boy continues:

"Is it because they're going to come today that you took it off?"

"How do you know they're going to come today?"

"My mother . . ." the boy begins; but he goes no further.

To say something, the soldier asks: "And she lets you run around the streets?"

"I don't run around. There was an errand to do."

"Is she the one who sent you?"

The child hesitates. He looks at the soldier as if he were trying to guess what is coming next, where he is being led to, what kind of trap is being set for him.

"No," he says finally, "she's not."

"So it was your father?" the soldier asks.

This time the boy decides not to answer. The soldier himself has been speaking more slowly during the last few remarks. The slight animation the wine had given him has already vanished, and his fatigue gradually masters him again. Probably he still has fever; the effect of the pills has not lasted long. Nevertheless he continues, his voice lower:

"I ran into him this morning, I think, as I was leaving the barracks. He does pretty well on his bad leg. Yes, I'm sure that's who it was. So he wasn't at home . . ."

"He's not my father," the child says, and he turns his head toward the door.

The two workers at the next table have broken off their conversation, perhaps some time ago. The man whose back was turned has pivoted on his chair without letting go of his glass or raising it from the table, and he has remained in this position, his body half turned to look behind him toward the soldier, or toward the child. The latter has moved away. At least he is now some distance from the soldier to the left, near the wall where the white bulletins are posted announcing the military evacuation of the city. Complete silence has fallen in the room.

The soldier has remained in the same position: his elbows and forearms in front of him, his grease-spotted hands lying near each other about four inches apart, the right hand still holding the empty glass.

The bartender, a tall, thickset figure, has returned to the room and is standing behind his bar at the far right. He is motionless too, leaning slightly forward, his arms wide apart, his hands grasping the edge of the bar. He too is looking at the soldier, or at the child.

The child has put his beret back on his head. He has pulled both sides far down in order to cover his ears as much as possible, and he has pulled the cape around his body, holding it closed with both hands from inside. At the other end of the room, the bartender has not moved either. When he served the soldier just now, he told him that when he had first seen him through the glass, then crossing the threshold, he had taken him, in this city where no soldiers circulated any longer, and where everyone expected to see the newcomers appear at any moment— he had taken him for one of the latter. But this was only the effect of surprise, and once the soldier had come in, the bartender had immediately recognized the familiar uniform with the long overcoat and the leggings.

The boy had then closed the door behind this unexpected customer. The bartender standing at his post, the customer in middle-class clothes standing near the counter, the two workers sitting at their table, all stared at him without saying anything. It was the boy who had broken the silence, his low voice sounding so little like a child's that the soldier had supposed one of the four men watching him come in had spoken. The child was still standing near the door at this moment, behind him. But the others facing him remained motionless, mouths closed, lips motionless; and the sentence, without some-one to have spoken it, seemed to be a title underneath a picture.

Afterward the soldier, his glass of wine finished, has remained no longer in this silent café. He has picked up his package from under his chair and has left the room, accompanied as far as the door by the stares of the bartender and the two workers. After quickly readjusting the distended white string, he has put the package wrapped in brown paper back under his left arm.

Outside, the cold has shocked him once again. This overcoat must not be as thick as the other, unless the temperature has dropped a great deal during the night. The snow, hardened by repeated trampling, grates under his hobnail boots. The soldier walks faster in order to warm himself; urged on by the regularity of the noise his boots make as he walks, he advances without looking where he is going, as though aimlessly, through the deserted streets. When he decided to continue on his way, it was because of the notion that there still remained something to be done in order to get the box to its proper recipient. But when he found himself on the side-walk again, having closed the café door behind him, he no longer knew which way to turn: he simply tried to proceed to the first meeting place (where he had not been met), without, moreover, losing any time thinking out the best way to get to it, since the man was no longer waiting for him there, now, in any case. The soldier's only hope is that the man lives in the vicinity and that he will meet him on his way. At the first crossroad he has found the lame man again.

Approaching the crossroad where the man is standing, at the corner of the last house, he realizes that it is not the lame man but the man in middle-class clothes who was drinking at the bar just now; he is not leaning on a crutch, but on an umbrella which he is holding in front of him, its tip stuck in the hard snow. His body leans forward slightly. He is wearing spats over his well polished shoes, narrow trousers, and a short overcoat which is probably fur-lined. He has no hat on his head, which is bald in front.

Just before the soldier reaches him, the man bows quickly, his umbrella remaining stuck at an angle in the snow in front of him. The material of the umbrella, rolled tight, is protected by a black silk sheath.

The soldier answers the bow with a nod and attempts to continue on his way, but the other man makes a gesture with his free hand, and the soldier imagines that the man is about to speak to him. He turns toward him and stands still, raising his eyebrows with the look of someone expecting to be spoken to. The man, as if he had foreseen nothing of the kind, then lowers his eyes toward the end of his umbrella stuck at an angle in the hard yellow snow. Yet he has kept his left arm half raised, elbow bent, hand open, thumb up. On his third finger he is wearing a heavy signet ring with a gray stone in it.

"Nasty weather, isn't it?" he says at last, and turns his head toward the soldier. The latter thus finds his expectation justified: he has the feeling again, very distinctly, that this little remark is only a prelude to more personal information. He therefore merely answers it by a vague acquiescence, a kind of grumble. He is still preparing to listen to what follows.

There is a considerable lapse of time, nevertheless, before the man with the umbrella and the fur-lined coat makes up his mind to ask: "Are you looking for something?" Is this the signal?

"I was supposed to meet . . ." the solder begins.

Since the rest is too long in coming, the other man finishes the sentence himself: "Someone who never showed up?"

"Yes," the soldier says. "It was yesterday

. . . I mean the day before yesterday . . . It was supposed to be at noon . . ."

"And you came too late?"

"Yes . . . No. I must have come to the wrong place. A street corner . . ."

"It was a crossroads like this one? Under a lamppost?"

A black lamppost, its base embossed with a garland of stylized ivy whose pattern the snow accentuates . . . Immediately the soldier goes into a more detailed explanation; but no sooner has he begun than he is overcome by doubt and decides to confine himself, out of caution, to a series of incoherent phrases without apparent connection, for the most part incomplete and in any case quite obscure to his interlocutor, in which he himself, moreover, becomes more involved at each word. The other man does not show any sign that his attention is flagging; he listens with polite interest, his eyes squinting slightly, his head tilted to the left, showing no more comprehension than astonishment.

The soldier no longer knows how to stop. He has taken his right hand out of his pocket and moves it forward, clenching his fingers like someone afraid of losing some detail of a memory he thinks he is about to recapture, or like someone who wants to be encouraged, or who does not

manage to be convincing, and he continues talking, losing himself in a plethora of increasingly
confusing specifications, suddenly conscious of
this, stopping at almost each step in order to
start again in a different direction, convinced
now, but too late, of having blundered from the
beginning, and not seeing any means of extricat-
ing himself without planting still deeper suspicions in this anonymous pedestrian who merely
mentioned the temperature or some banal subject of the sort, or who even asked him nothing
at all—and who, moreover, continues to say
nothing.

Even while struggling in his own nets, the
soldier tries to reconstitute what has just happened: it must have occurred to him (but this
now seems incredible) that the man he has been
running after since his arrival in the city was
perhaps this very man, with his silk-sheathed
umbrella, his fur-lined coat, his big ring. He has
wanted to allude to what he expected of him,
yet without revealing his true mission, permitting the man, all the same, to determine it, if he
was actually the man for whom the box wrapped
in brown paper was intended, or at least the man
who could say what must be done with it.

The man in gray spats and shiny black shoes,
on the contrary, no longer gave the slightest sign
of complicity. The ringed hand had even fallen

back and eventually returned to the coat pocket. The right hand, the one holding the handle of the umbrella, was wearing a dark-gray leather glove. The soldier supposed for a moment that this man was keeping silent on purpose: that he was, in fact, the recipient in question but refusing to make himself known, and that having learned what he himself wanted to know he was concealing his identity . . . This was obviously absurd. Either the business had nothing to do with him or else he had not yet realized that what the soldier was trying to tell him was of the greatest importance to him. Since he had not immediately clutched at this straw being offered to him, the soldier had to choose between two solutions: to speak more openly or else to beat an immediate retreat. But he had not had time to choose one course or the other, and he had persisted in both directions at once, which further risked discouraging his interlocutor if he were, in spite of everything, etc. . . .

The soldier must finally have fallen silent, for they are now standing opposite each other again, frozen in the same position as at the start: the soldier has both hands in his overcoat pockets and stares obliquely at the man in the fur-lined coat who half extends his gloveless left hand, a signet ring with a gray stone on the ring finger, while in his right hand he holds his umbrella at arm's length, stuck at an angle in front of him into the hard-packed snow on the sidewalk. About three yards behind him is the cast-iron lamppost, a former gas light with old-fashioned ornamentation, now equipped with an electric bulb that shines with a yellowish luster in the leaden daylight.

Yet the man has derived some information from the soldier's fragmentary and contradictory stammerings, for after a moment's thought, probably quite a long moment, he asks: "Then someone was supposed to meet you not far from here?" And he adds a moment later, as though to himself: "A man, in the street, these last few days."

Then without waiting for confirmation or asking a complementary question, he begins explaining that he himself, it seems most likely, has seen the person in question: a bare-headed man of medium height, wearing a long brown coat, who was standing at the foot of a corner apartment house. He had noticed him there on several occasions—at least two—when he had passed by: this morning, yesterday as well, and even the day before perhaps. This solitary person, dressed in dark brown, who had been standing in the snow for a long time judging by his position—his hip and shoulder leaning against the cast-iron shaft like a man who is tired of standing—yes, he remembered perfectly having noticed him.

"How old?" the soldier asks.

"About thirty . . . or forty."

"No," the soldier says, "that wasn't the one. He was supposed to be over fifty and dressed in black . . . And why would he have come back like that, several days in a row?"

The last argument hardly stands up, he realizes, for he himself has returned on many occasions, as a matter of fact—and again this morning—to what he supposed was the meeting place, however variable. Moreover, his interlocutor points out that a change in the clothes agreed upon might have been compelled by the snow then falling so thickly; as for the age, he is not certain of that, having glimpsed this figure at some distance, especially the second time.

"Besides," the soldier says, "it might have been me."

But the man assures him he would not have confused an infantry uniform with civilian clothes. He urges the soldier to examine the place he indicates, at least to give it a look: it is so close by it is worth the trouble, particularly if the matter is an important one.

"That box you have under your arm, you were saying it . . ."

"No," the soldier interrupts. "That has nothing to do with it."

Since he has virtually no other resources, he decides, despite his certainty of the uselessness of such a procedure, to go to the crossroads in question: he must turn right at the third street, then go to the end of the block of houses, if not to the next cross street. He has set off without turning back, leaving the stranger behind him still leaning on his umbrella. This prolonged delay has frozen his body through. Although all his joints are numb with fever and fatigue, he experiences a kind of relief in walking again, particularly since he has the prospect of a precise and not too distant goal. Once he has ascertained the futility of this last hope (which is not even that), there will be nothing left to do but get rid of his burdensome package.

It would obviously be best to destroy it, the contents in any case, since the box itself is made of iron. But if it is easy to burn the papers inside it, or to tear them up into tiny pieces, there are also other objects more difficult to tear up—the exact nature of which, moreover, he has never checked. He will have to get rid of the whole thing. To throw away the package without even unwrapping it would be the simplest solution from every point of view. As he crosses a side street, the soldier happens to notice a sewer mouth in front of him near the rounded curb of the sidewalk. He approaches it and, despite the stiffness of his joints, leans down in order to make sure the box is not too large to pass through the arched opening in the stone curb. Fortunately the layer of snow is not thick enough to impede the operation. The box will just fit. All he needs to do is to push it through horizontally until it falls over onto the other side. Why not get rid of it right away?

At the last minute, the soldier cannot make up his mind to do it. Having reassured himself by twice checking that the operation can be accomplished without difficulty, he straightens up at the crucial moment and begins walking straight ahead in order to look over there first, to see whether by some chance . . . But the mere fact of having to step over the curb of the sidewalk, some eight inches, keeps him motionless for a moment, so greatly has the insignificant effort he has just made exhausted him.

As soon as he stops moving, the cold becomes unbearable. He crosses the gutter and takes another two steps. Suddenly he is so exhausted that he can manage to go no farther. He leans his hip and shoulder against the cast-iron shaft of the street light. Was it here that he was supposed to turn right? To see if the man with the gray ring has not remained where he was, leaning forward on his umbrella, in order to show him from a distance the place where he is supposed to turn, the soldier glances behind him. Twenty yards away, walking in his tracks, is the boy.

The soldier, who has immediately turned his head away, has begun walking again. After five or six steps he looks behind him again. The boy is following him. If he were able to, the soldier would begin running. But he is completely exhausted. And probably this child has nothing against him. The soldier stops and turns around once again.

The boy has stopped too, his wide, serious eyes staring at the soldier. He no longer has his beret on his head. He is no longer holding his cape closed around him.

The soldier now moves toward the boy, almost without moving his body, his steps extremely slow, as if he were frozen stiff. The boy does not back away.

"Do you have something to tell me?" the soldier asks in a tone of voice meant to be threatening but which scarcely escapes his lips.

"Yes," the boy answers.

However he does not say anything more.

The soldier looks at the snow-covered stoop two yards to his right, beneath a closed door. He would feel the cold less if he could take shelter in the doorway. He takes a step. He murmurs:

"Well, I'm going to sit down a little."

Having reached the doorway, he leans in the corner, half against the wood, half against the stone jamb.

The child has pivoted to watch the soldier. He has opened his mouth slightly. He examines the face with the black growth of beard, the body slumped backward, the package, the heavy boots a few inches apart on the stoop. Gradually the soldier lets himself slide down against the door, bending his knees until he is sitting in the snow which has accumulated in the right side of the doorway on the narrow stoop.

"Why did you want to throw away your box?" the child says.

"No, I . . . I wasn't going to throw it away."

"Then what were you doing?"

His low voice is now without mistrust, his questions are not hostile.

"I wanted to see," the soldier says.

"To see? . . . To see what?"

"If it would go through."

But the child does not seem to be convinced. He grasps the edges of his open cape, one in each hand, and sways his arms in cadence, back and forth, back and forth. The cold still does not seem to bother him. At the same time, without coming any closer, he continues his careful scrutiny: the brown package now hugged between chest and thighs, the overcoat collar with the insignia removed, the legs bent, the knees pointing under the flaps of khaki material.

"Your coat," he says at last, "isn't the same as yesterday."

"Yesterday . . . Did you see me yesterday?"

"Of course. I've seen you every day. Your coat was dirty . . . Did they clean it for you?"

"No . . . Yes, I guess so."

The child pays no attention to the answer.

"You don't know how to wrap your leggings," he says.

"All right . . . you'll teach me."

The child shrugs his shoulders. The soldier, exhausted by the conversation, fears still more that his companion will run away, abandoning him in the empty street where night will soon fall. Is it not the same boy who has already taken him to a café that was still open and to a barracks dormitory? The soldier forces himself to ask in a friendlier tone of voice:

"Was that what you wanted to tell me?"

"No," the boy answers, "that wasn't it."

Then they heard the distant sound of the motorcycle.

No. It was something else. It is dark. There is another attack, the dry, staccato sound of automatic rifles quite close behind the little woods, and on the other side too, now and then, against a low, rumbling background. The dirt path is now as soft as if it had been plowed. The wounded man grows heavier and heavier, can no longer lift his shoes, is unable to walk any farther. He must be supported and dragged at the same time. Both men have abandoned their knapsacks. The wounded man has also dropped his rifle, but the other man has kept his, although its strap has broken and he is forced to carry it in his hand. It would have been better to take another one: there was no lack of rifles to choose from. He has preferred to keep the one he was accustomed to, though it is useless and awkward. He carries it horizontally, in his left hand. His right arm is around the waist of his wounded comrade, whose left arm is crooked around his neck. In the darkness they stumble at each step on the soft earth; there are many ruts and furrows, and only fleeting gleams of light.

Afterwards he walks alone. He has neither knapsack nor rifle nor comrade to carry any more. All he is carrying now is the box wrapped in brown paper under his left arm. He advances through the night across the fresh snow covering the ground, and his footsteps appear one after the other in the thin, uniform layer of snow, making a sound regular as clockwork. Having reached the crossroads under the yellow light of the street light, he approaches the gutter and bends down, one foot on the edge of the sidewalk, the other in the street. The stone arch of a sewer mouth appears between his stiff legs; he bends over farther and holds the box toward the black opening, where it immediately disappears, swallowed up by the void.

The next image shows the dormitory of a barracks, or more precisely, of a military hospital. The rectangular box, which is the size and shape of a shoe box, is lying on the kit shelf next to an aluminum cup, a mess-tin, some neatly folded khaki clothes, and various other small objects. Beneath, in the white-painted metal bed, a man is lying on his back. His eyes are closed; the lids are gray, as are the forehead and the temples; but the two cheekbones are bright pink; over the hollow cheeks, around the half-open mouth, and across the chin there is a black beard of four or five days' growth. The sheet, pulled up to his chin, rises periodically with the wounded man's slightly wheezing respiration. One reddish hand sticks out of the brown blankets on one side and hangs over the edge of the mattress.

To the right and left, other bodies are lying on other identical beds lined up against one bare wall, along which, a yard above their heads, is attached the shelf filled with knapsacks, wooden boxes, folded clothes either khaki or olive drab, and aluminum dishes and cups. A little farther along among the toilet utensils is a large round alarm clock—doubtless stopped—whose hands indicate a quarter to four.

In the next room, a considerable crowd has gathered: men standing, mostly in civilian clothes, talking in small groups and making many gestures. The soldier tries to clear a path but without success. Suddenly someone he saw only from the rear, standing in his way, turns around and motionlessly stares at him, his eyes squinting slightly, as though with a great effort of attention. Gradually the men nearby turn to look at him, all suddenly motionless, silent, squinting slightly. He soon finds himself in the center of a circle which grows progressively larger as the figures step back, only their pale faces still visible, farther and farther apart, at equal intervals, like a series of street lights along a straight street. The row sways slightly, becoming a receding perspective: the shafts of black cast-iron stand out sharply against the snow. In front of the nearest one is the boy, who stares at him wide-eyed:

"Why are you staying there like that?" he says. "Are you sick?"

The soldier makes an effort to answer:

"I'll be all right."

"Did you lose your barracks again?"

"No . . . I'm going back now."

"Why don't you wear a cap? All the soldiers wear caps . . . or helmets."

After a pause, the child continues, his voice still lower: "My father has a helmet."

"Where is your father?"

"I don't know." Then loudly, carefully articulating each word: "It's not true that he deserted."

The soldier looks up at the boy again: "Who says he did?"

In answer, the child takes a few steps with a limping gait, his legs stiff, one arm stretched alongside his body, grasping a crutch. He is now only a yard away from the door. He continues:

"But it's not true. And he said you're a spy. You're not a real soldier: you're a spy. There's a bomb in your package."

"Well, that's not true either," the soldier says.

Now they have heard the distant sound of the motorcycle. The boy has cocked his head first; he has opened his mouth a little wider and his head has gradually pivoted from street light to street light toward the gray end of the street, already vague in the twilight. Now he has looked at the soldier and then at the end of the street again, while the noise was growing rapidly louder. It was the sputtering of a two-cylinder motor. The child has drawn back toward the doorway.

But the noise has begun to diminish, soon becoming almost inaudible.

"I have to go back," the child says.

He has looked at the soldier and repeated: "I have to go back home."

He has approached the soldier, he has held out his hand. Hesitating at first, the soldier has grasped his hand and has managed to stand up, leaning one shoulder against the door.

The same sputtering of a motor has begun again in the silence, swelling in volume, this time much more distinctly. The man and the child have stepped back together into the doorway. The noise has soon come so close that they have stepped up onto the stoop and are flattened against the wood of the door beside each other. The staccato racket echoing in all directions against the housefronts unmistakably came from the adjacent street, the one forming the crossroads some ten yards from their hiding place. They have flattened themselves even more against the door. The motorcycle has appeared at the edge of the vertical wall, at the corner of the house. It was a side car with two helmeted soldiers in it; it was advancing slowly down the middle of the street, in the fresh snow.

The two men appear in profile. The driver's face, situated slightly forward, is above his companion's. They seem to have the same features:

regular, drawn, perhaps shrunken by fatigue. Their eyes are hollow, their lips tight, their skin grayish. The color and shape of their jackets are like those of the familiar uniform, but the helmet is larger, heavier, protecting the ears and the back of the neck. The motorcycle itself is dirty and half covered with dry mud; it seems to be a rather old model. The man driving it sits stiffly on his seat, his gloved hands grasping the handle bars. The other man looks alternately right and left, but only ahead of the motorcycle, almost without moving his head. On his knees he holds a black machine gun whose barrel sticks out of the iron-plated car.

They have passed without turning back and have continued straight ahead past the cross-road. After about twenty yards, they have disappeared behind the corner of the apartment house forming the opposite corner.

A few seconds later the sound has suddenly stopped. Apparently the motor was turned off. Complete silence followed the racket. There remained only the two parallel lines left in the snow by the three wheels of the vehicle, drawn straight across the field of vision between the two planes of vertical stone.

Since this was taking too long, the child has lost patience and has left his hiding place. The soldier has not noticed this immediately, for previously the child had been huddled behind him; the soldier has just seen him in the middle of the sidewalk and has gestured to him to come back. But the child has taken another three steps forward, so that he is now standing against the street light, which is supposed to conceal him.

The silence persisted. The boy, who quickly grew bolder as time passed, has advanced several yards towards the crossroads. For fear of attracting the attention of the invisible motorcyclists, the soldier has not dared call him to keep him from going farther. The child has continued to the point from which he can see the entire cross street; sticking his head out, he has glanced in the direction the side car had vanished. A man's voice, some distance away, in this area, has shouted a short command. With a start, the child has turned around and begun running; he has passed the soldier again, his cape fluttering over his shoulders. Before realizing what he was doing, the soldier was already following him when the two-cylinder motor started up again, suddenly filling the air with its sputtering. The soldier too has begun running, laboriously, while the child has turned the corner of the next street.

Behind him, the racket has quickly become deafening. Then came a long grating sound: the motorcycle taking too sharp a turn and skidding on the snow. At the same time the motor stopped. The harsh voice shouted: "Halt!" twice, without the slightest trace of an accent. The soldier almost reached the corner of the street where the child himself had turned a few seconds before. The motorcycle has started up again, drowning out the powerful voice which was repeating "Halt!" for the third time. And immediately afterwards, the soldier recognized the dry staccato crackling of the machine gun which mingled with the uproar.

He has felt a violent shock on the heel of his right boot. He has kept on running. Bullets have struck the stone wall near him. Just as he was turning the corner, there was a new burst of firing. A sharp pain has pierced his left side. Then everything stopped.

He was out of reach, protected by the wall. The crackling of the machine gun had stopped. The motor had probably stopped a few seconds before. The soldier no longer felt his body, he was still running along the stone wall. The apartment house door was not closed, it opened easily when the soldier pushed it. He has gone in. He has closed it behind him gently; the bolt, as it falls back into place, has made a slight click.

Afterward he lay down on the floor in the darkness, curling up with the box in the hollow of his stomach. He has felt the back of his boot:

there was a deep diagonal rent along the back and side of the heel. His foot was not touched. Heavy steps and noisy voices have echoed in the street.

The steps drew closer. A muffled blow has resounded against the wood of the door, then the voices again, rough, rather jovial, speaking an incomprehensible language with drawling intonations. The noise of one man's steps has faded away. The two voices, one quite near, the other somewhat farther away, have exchanged three or four short sentences. Someone has knocked on something, probably another door, and on this one again, with a fist, several times, but apparently without conviction. The more distant voice has shouted foreign words again and the nearer voice has begun laughing loudly. Then the other voice burst into laughter too.

And the two heavy treads have faded away together, accompanied by bursts of laughter. In the ensuing silence the sound of the motorcycle has begun again, then gradually diminished until it is no longer audible.

The soldier has wanted to change position. A sharp pain has pierced his side. A very violent but not unbearable pain. Most of all he was tired. And he felt like vomiting.

Then he heard the boy's low voice quite near him in the darkness, but he did not understand what it was saying. He felt he was losing consciousness.

A considerable crowd has gathered in the room: men, mostly in civilian clothes, talking in small groups and making many gestures. The soldier tries to make his way through them. He finally reaches a less crowded area where the people sitting at tables are drinking wine and arguing, still with many gestures and exclamations. The tables are very close together and circulation between the benches, chairs, and human backs is still difficult; but it is easier to see where one is going. Unfortunately all the chairs seem to be occupied. The tables—round, square, or rectangular—are set facing in every direction, without discernible order. Some have no more than three or four drinkers around them; the larger ones, which are long and have benches, can serve fifteen. Beyond is the bar behind which the bartender is standing, a tall, heavy-set man, made even more noticeable by his slightly raised position. Between the bar and the last tables, a very narrow space is obstructed in the center by a group of standing drinkers who are more luxuriously dressed in short overcoats or fur-collared cloaks, and whose glasses,

set down within arm's reach in front of the bartender, are partially visible in the openings left
here and there between the bodies and the arms
in their demonstrative attitudes. One of these
men, to the right and a little to the rear, instead
of participating in his friends' conversation, is
leaning back against the edge of the bar in order
to look at the room, the seated drinkers, the
soldier.

The latter finally glimpses, not far away, a
small, relatively accessible table at which only
two other soldiers are sitting: an infantry corporal and a cavalry corporal. Motionless and silent, both men's reserved appearance contrasts
with that of the men around them. There is an
unoccupied chair between them.

Having succeeded in reaching it without too
much difficulty, the soldier rests one hand on its
back and asks if he may sit down. It is the infantry corporal who replies: they were with a
friend, but the latter, who has gone away for
a minute, doesn't seem to be coming back; he
has probably met someone he knows somewhere
else. Why not take his place until he comes back.
This is what the soldier does, pleased to find a
seat free.

The two others say nothing. They are not
drinking; they do not even have glasses in front
of them. The racket of the room around them

does not seem to affect them; they keep their eyes fixed straight ahead, as though they were sleeping without lowering their lids. If not, they are certainly not both looking so fixedly at the same thing, for the man on the right is facing the left wall, which is quite bare at this point, since the white bulletins are posted farther forward, and the man on the opposite side is facing the bar.

Halfway from the bar, over which the bartender's thickset body is leaning between his widespread arms, a young waitress is passing among the tables with her loaded tray. At least she is looking around to find a place where she is needed: having stopped for a moment, she pivots in order to glance in all directions; she moves neither her feet, her legs, nor the lower part of her body beneath the full-pleated skirt, but only her head (with its black hair in a heavy bun) and the upper part of her body; her two outstretched arms, which are holding the tray at eye level, leave the latter in virtually the same place when she turns in the other direction, remaining twisted in this way for some time.

Judging from the direction of her gaze, the soldier supposes she has noticed his presence and will therefore approach this newcomer's table to take his order, or even that she will serve him at once, for on her tray she is carrying a bottle of red wine which, moreover, she is tilting dangerously, at the risk of letting it fall off the tray, which she is not keeping horizontal. But below, in the trajectory of an imminent fall, the old, bald worker apparently suspects nothing, continuing to address the man at his right, or appealing to him, or calling him to witness, while brandishing in his right hand his still full glass, whose contents are on the point of spilling.

The soldier then remembers that there is not one glass on his own table. Yet the tray holds only the one bottle and nothing which might satisfy a new customer in the way of a glass. The waitress, moreover, has not discovered anything to attract her attention in this area, and her glance now completes its circuit of the room, having passed the soldier and his two companions, now sweeping over the other tables along the wall where the small white bulletins are attached by four tacks, then the window with its pleated curtain at eye level and its three enamel balls outside the glass, then the door, also partially curtained and with the word "Café" showing in reverse, then the bar in front of it with the five or six men in middle-class clothes, and at the far right the last of these men who is still looking toward the soldier's table.

The latter continues staring straight ahead.

The cavalry corporal now fixes his eyes on the collar of the soldier's coat where the two diamonds of green felt showing the serial number are sewn.

"So you were at Reichenfels?" And at the same time his chin points forward with a short, quick movement.

The soldier replies: "Yes, I was in the area."

"You were there," the cavalry corporal corrects, repeating his gesture as though to prove the fact by indicating the regiment's distinctive insignia.

"The other one was too," the infantry corporal says. "The man who was sitting here just now."

"But he did some fighting," the cavalry corporal snaps.

Then, since he receives no answer: "I hear there were some who weren't up to it."

He turns toward the cavalry corporal who makes a vague gesture of ignorance or agreement.

"No one was up to it," the soldier says.

But the cavalry corporal protests: "Yes, some were! Ask the little guy who was sitting here before."

"Maybe you're right," the soldier admits, "it all depends what you mean by 'up to it.'"

"I mean what it means. There were some who fought and some who didn't."

"They all got out of it eventually."

"They were ordered to! Keep it straight."

"Everyone stopped fighting on orders," the soldier says.

The cavalry corporal shrugs his shoulders. He looks at the infantry corporal as though he had expected support from him. Then he turns toward the large window looking out on the street. He murmurs: "Rotten officers!"

And again, after a few seconds: "Rotten officers, that's what it was."

"I'm with you there," the infantry corporal agrees.

The soldier tries to see, to his right or farther back, if the young waitress has not started to come over to their table, but even though he half rises from his chair to see over the heads of the drinkers surrounding it, he cannot catch sight of her anywhere.

"Don't worry," the infantry corporal says, "you'll see him soon enough when he comes back." He smiles rather pleasantly and adds, still supposing that the soldier is looking for the absent friend: "He must be over there, in the poolroom. He must have found someone he knew."

"You can ask him," the cavalry corporal continues with a thrust of his chin. "He was in the fighting. You can ask him."

"All right," the soldier says, "but he's here all the same, now. He had to come here just like everyone else."

"He was ordered to, I tell you," and after a moment of silent reflection he concludes, as though to himself, "Rotten officers, that's what it was!"

"I'm with you there," the infantry corporal agrees.

The soldier asks: "Were you at Reichenfels?"

"Oh, no," the infantry corporal answers, "we were both farther west. We fell back to keep from being taken when they broke through from the rear."

"We were ordered to. Remember that. Keep it straight," the cavalry corporal corrects.

"And we moved fast," the infantry corporal says. "It was no use hanging around: the twenty-eighth, on our left flank, waited too long and got picked off like flies."

"Anyway," the soldier says, "it all comes down to the same thing now. Sooner or later they'll get us."

The cavalry corporal glances at him, but prefers to address his remarks to an imaginary interlocutor sitting on the opposite side: "Nobody's proved that. We're not through yet."

Now the soldier shrugs his shoulders. This time he stands up completely to try to attract the waitress' attention and get something to drink. As he does so, he overhears a random sentence from the conversation at the next table: "I tell you there are spies everywhere!" A relative silence follows this declaration. Then, from the other end of the same table, comes a longer commentary in which only the words "firing squad" can be heard. The rest is lost in the general confusion. And another phrase stands out just as the soldier sits down again: "Some fought, others didn't."

The cavalry corporal immediately begins examining the green diamonds on the soldier's overcoat collar. He repeats: "We're not through yet." Then, leaning toward the infantry corporal, he says as though in confidence: "They say there are enemy agents paid to sabotage morale."

The other man shows no reaction. The cavalry corporal, who has vainly expected a reply, leaning forward across the red-and-white checked oilcloth, finally straightens up in his chair. A little later he says again: "Should take a look," but without explaining himself further, and in so low a tone that he can scarcely be heard. Both men are now silent, motionless, each one staring straight ahead into space.

The soldier has left them, intending to find

the young woman with the heavy dark hair. Yet once he is on his feet among the crowded tables, he has decided he was not so thirsty after all.

On the point of leaving, already not far from the bar and the group of middle-class drinkers, he has just remembered the soldier who was also at Reichenfels and who, for one, had fought so gloriously. The important thing was to find him, to talk to him, make him tell his story. The soldier immediately turns around and crosses the room in the opposite direction between the benches, the chairs, and the backs of the seated drinkers. The two men are still alone in the same positions in which he left them. Instead of proceeding to their table, he turns directly toward the back of the room to reach an area where everyone is standing: a crowd of men gesturing and shouldering each other toward the left, but advancing very slowly because of the narrowness of the passage, which they nevertheless gradually approach, between a projecting angle of the wall and three large, loaded, circular coat racks standing at the end of the bar. While the soldier too is moving forward along with the crowd—even more slowly since he is on the edge —he wonders why it suddenly seemed so urgent to talk to this man who could only tell him what he already knows. Before reaching the next room where there are probably more drinkers, a pool table concealed under its tarpaulin cover, the black-haired waitress, and the hero of Reichenfels, he has given up his project.

It is probably here that the scene occurs: the silent gathering which steps back in every direction around him, the soldier finally remaining alone in the center of a huge circle of pale faces . . . But this scene leads to nothing. Besides, the soldier is no longer in the center of a crowd, neither silent nor noisy; he has left the café and is walking in the street. It is an ordinary kind of street; long, straight, lined with identical houses with flat façades and uniform doors and windows. It is snowing, as usual, in close, small, slow flakes. The sidewalks are white, as are the street, the window sills, the stoops.

When a door is not closed tight, the snow which the wind drove into the doorway during the night has been wedged into the narrow vertical slit for several inches, remaining caked against the jamb when the soldier opens the door wide. A little snow has even accumulated inside, forming on the ground a long, tapering streak which has partially melted, leaving a moist black border on the dusty wood of the floor. Other black marks occur along the hallway at intervals of about two feet, growing fainter as they continue toward the staircase, whose first steps appear at the end of the hallway. Although the shape of these puddles is uncertain, change-able, and occasionally fringed with intermediary zones, it is likely that they are footprints left by small shoes.

On the right of the hallway as on the left are lateral doors at equal and alternating inter-vals, one to the right, one to the left, one to the right, etc. . . . The series continues as far as the eye can see, or almost, for the first steps of the staircase are still visible at the end of the hallway, lit by a brighter gleam. A small sil-houette, a woman or a child greatly reduced by the considerable distance, rests one hand on the large white sphere where the banister ends.

The more the soldier advances, the more he has the impression that this figure is retreating. But one of the doors has been opened on the right. Here, moreover, the footprints stop. Click. Darkness. Click. Yellow light revealing a narrow vestibule. Click. Darkness. Click. The soldier is once more in the square room furnished with a chest, a table, and a day bed. The table is cov-ered with a checkered oilcloth. Above the chest the photograph of a soldier in battle dress is fastened to the wall. Instead of sitting at the table drinking wine and slowly chewing his bread, the soldier is lying on the bed; his eyes are closed, he seems to be sleeping. Around him are standing three motionless people, who are looking at him without speaking: a man, a woman, and a child.

Right next to his face, at the head of the bed, the woman is bending forward slightly, examining the sleeper's drawn features, listening to his laborious breathing. Behind her, near the table, stands the boy, still wearing his black cape and beret. At the foot of the bed, the third person is not the lame man with the wooden crutch, but the older man whose head is bald in front, wearing a short fur-lined overcoat and well-polished shoes protected by spats. He has kept his fine gray leather gloves on; the one on his left hand is distended, on the third finger, by the stone of his signet ring. The umbrella must have remained in the vestibule leaning against the coat rack, with its ivory handle and its silk sheath.

The soldier is lying on his back, fully dressed, with his leggings and his heavy boots. His arms are at his sides. His overcoat is unbuttoned; underneath it, his uniform jacket is spotted with blood on the left side, near the waist.

No. Actually it is another wounded man who occupies the scene, outside the door of the busy café. The soldier has no sooner closed the door behind him than he sees a young man coming toward him, a soldier drafted the year before whom he has met several times during the retreat and again this morning at the hospital, who is also about to go into the café. For a second, the soldier imagines he has before his eyes the valiant fighter referred to inside, the man whose conduct the cavalry corporal had just been praising. He immediately realizes the impossibility of such a coincidence: the young man happened to be at Reichenfels during the enemy attack, but in his own regiment, as the green diamonds on his uniform attest; yet this unit did not include a single hero, as the cavalry corporal had clearly implied. As the soldier is about to pass his comrade, merely nodding to him, the latter stops to speak to him: "Your friend you went to see this morning in surgery," he says, "is pretty bad. He's been asking for you several times."

"All right," the soldier says. "I'll go back."

"You better hurry. He won't last long."

The young man has already put his hand on the brass doorknob when he turns to add: "He says he's got something to give you." After a moment's thought: "But maybe it's just delirium."

"I'll go see," the soldier says.

He immediately begins walking quickly, taking the shortest route. The setting he passes through is no longer that of the great symmetrical and monotonous city with its straight roads intersecting each other at right angles. And there is no snow yet. The weather is even rather mild, for the season. The houses are low, old-fashioned, vaguely baroque, over-ornamented with volutes, molded cornices, columns with carved capitals framing the doors, balconies with sculptured brackets, complicated cast-iron railings. All of which corresponds to the lampposts on the street corners, former gas lights that have been converted, consisting of a cast-iron column widening at the base and supporting, three yards from the ground, a lyre-shaped structure with twining branches, from which is suspended the globe containing the large electric bulb. The shaft itself is not uniform, but girdled with many rings of varying shapes and sizes, indicating at various heights changes in diameter, swellings, constrictions, circular or spindle-shaped bulges; these rings are particularly numerous toward the top of the cone which constitutes the foot of the structure; around this cone spirals a garland of stylized ivy embossed on the metal and reproduced identically on each lamppost.

But the hospital is only a military building of classic construction, at the rear of a large, bare, gravel courtyard separated from the boulevard and its leafless trees by a high iron fence whose gate is wide open. On each side the sentry boxes are empty. In the center of the huge courtyard one man is standing, a non-commissioned officer with belted tunic and kepi; he is standing perfectly still. He seems to be thinking; his black shadow lies at his feet across the white gravel.

As for the room where the wounded man is, it is an ordinary hall whose metal beds have been painted white—a decor which also leads to nothing, if not to the box wrapped in brown paper lying on the kit shelf.

Hence it is with this box under his arm that the soldier walks through the snowy streets along the high, flat housefronts when he is looking for the meeting place, hesitating among several similar crossroads, deciding that the description he has been furnished is quite inadequate to determine the exact place with any certainty in this huge city arranged so geometrically. And finally he goes back to an apparently uninhabited apartment house, pushing open a door that has remained ajar. The hallway, painted dark brown halfway up the wall, has the same deserted aspect as the streets themselves: doors with neither door mat nor calling card, absence of the usual household utensils left here or there which usually show that a house is inhabited, and walls completely bare save for the compulsory civil defense bulletin.

And then comes the side door which opens onto a narrow vestibule where the black-sheathed umbrella is leaning against an ordinary coat rack.

But another entrance makes it possible to

leave the apartment house without being seen
by someone watching for you at the doorway:
it opens onto the cross street at the end of the
secondary hallway perpendicular to the first, to
the left of the staircase ending the latter. Moreover, this street is in every way similar to the
preceding one; and the child is here at his post,
waiting for the soldier at the foot of the lamppost in order to lead him to the military offices
which serve as a kind of barracks and hospital.

In any case they have set out with this intention. However the crossroads and sudden
changes in direction increase in number, and
the interminable walk through the night continues. Since the boy goes faster and faster, the
soldier is soon no longer able to follow him and
is alone again, with no other recourse than to
seek some shelter in which to sleep. He doesn't
have much choice, and must content himself
with the first door he finds open. This is once
again the apartment of the young woman in the
gray apron with the black hair, the pale eyes,
the low voice. Yet he had not noticed, at first,
that the room where he had been given bread
and wine, under the framed photograph of the
husband in battle dress fastened to the wall over
the chest, contained a day bed as well as the
rectangular table covered with a checkered oilcloth.

At the top of the wall opposite this bed, almost at the angle of the ceiling, there is a small, sinuous black line a little over four inches long, which may be a crack in the plaster, perhaps a dusty spider web, perhaps merely a defect in the white paint emphasized by the harsh lighting of the electric light bulb hanging at the end of its wire swaying back and forth in a slow, oscillating movement. In the same rhythm, but in the opposite direction, the shadow of the man with the unsewn chevrons and the civilian trousers (is this the man whom the lame man called the lieutenant?), the shadow on the floor sways left and right against the closed door on either side of the motionless body.

This psuedo-lieutenant (but the insignia missing from his jacket were those of a corporal, their outline remaining clearly visible on the brown material), this man who took in the wounded or the sick must have first leaned out of a second floor window, probably the one just over the door, in order to try to see, in the darkness, who wanted to come in. However this does not resolve the main problem: how had he known that there was someone on the doorstep? Had the boy knocked on the closed door when he got there? Therefore, the soldier, having finally caught up with his guide after a considerable delay, since he had no longer been following

him for some time now save by his tracks, had
not suspected that his presence would already
be announced and that while he was perched
on the narrow stoop vainly trying to decipher
the inscription stamped on the polished plaque
by passing his fingertips back and forth across
it, his host, three yards above him, was minutely
observing part of his overcoat which stuck out
beyond the doorway: a shoulder, a stained sleeve
hugging a package whose shape and size resem-
bled those of a shoe box.

Yet no window was lighted, and the soldier
had thought this house, like the others, deserted
by its inhabitants. Having pushed open the door,
he had soon realized his error: a large number
of tenants were still there (as everywhere else,
too, no doubt), and appeared one after the other
on all sides, a young woman flattening herself at
the rear of the hallway against the corner of the
staircase, another woman suddenly opening her
door on the left, and finally a third, on the right,
revealing, after some hesitation, the vestibule
leading once again to the square room where the
soldier is now lying.

He is lying on his back. His eyes are closed.
The lids are gray, as are the forehead and the

temples, but the cheekbones are bright pink. Across the hollow cheeks, around the half open mouth and over the chin, there is a four or five days' growth of black beard. The sheet, pulled up to the chin, rises periodically with the slightly wheezing respiration. One reddish hand with black stains at the joints of the fingers sticks out at one side and hangs over the edge of the bed. Neither the man with the umbrella nor the boy is in the room any longer. Only the woman is here, sitting at the table, but at an angle, so that she is facing the soldier.

She is knitting a garment out of black wool; but her work is not yet far along. The heavy ball of yarn is lying near her on the red-and-white checked oilcloth which hangs over the edge of the table in wide, stiff folds at the corners. The rest of the room is not quite as the soldier has remembered it; not counting the day bed, whose presence he had scarcely noticed on his first visit, there is at least one important thing to be noted: a high window now completely concealed by long red curtains falling from ceiling to floor. Though wide, the day bed might easily have passed unnoticed, for it is placed in the corner concealed from the eyes of someone coming into the room by the open door; afterwards the soldier turned his back to it when he was eating and drinking at the table; and be-

sides, he was paying little attention to the furnishings, his senses dulled by fatigue, hunger,
and the cold outside. However he is surprised
that his eyes were not caught by what was then,
as now, just opposite him: the window, or in
any case the red curtains made of some thin
shiny material that resembles satin.

These curtains must not have been drawn;
for, as they look today, spread out under the
light, it is impossible not to be struck by their
color. Probably the window itself was then visible, between two narrow vertical red strips that
were not clearly lighted and so much less noticeable. But if it had been daylight, what did
this window look out on? Was it a street scene
which would appear through the panes of glass?
Given the monotony of the neighborhood, there
would certainly be nothing remarkable about
such a view. Or else it was something else: a
courtyard, perhaps, so narrow and dark on the
ground floor level that it provided little daylight
and no view of any interest, especially if thick
draperies kept whatever was outside from being
seen.

Despite these rationalizations, the soldier is
still perturbed by such a gap in his memory. He
wonders if anything else in his surroundings
might have escaped him and even continues to
escape him now. It suddenly seems very im-

portant to make an exact inventory of the room. There is the fireplace, about which he has remembered almost nothing: an ordinary black marble mantlepiece with a large rectangular mirror over it; its iron grate is open, revealing a heap of light gray ashes, but no andirons; on the mantlepiece is lying a rather long object, not very tall—only a half an inch, or an inch at the most—which cannot be identified from this angle, not being placed near enough the edge of the shelf (it is even possible that it is much wider than it looks); in the mirror are reflected the satiny red curtains whose folds gleam with vertical reflections . . . The soldier has the impression that all this is nothing: he must take note of other details in this room, details much more important than all the preceding ones, one detail in particular which he had been vaguely conscious of when he came into the room the other time, the day of the red wine and the slice of bread . . . He no longer remembers what it was. He wants to turn around in order to examine the chest more carefully. But he cannot manage to move except in the most insignificant way, a kind of torpor paralyzing his whole body. Only his hands and forearms move with any ease.

"You want something?" the young woman's low voice asks.

She has not changed position, having stopped in the middle of her work, her knitting still held in front of her, her fingers still placed—one forefinger raised, the other bent double—as if they were about to make a new stitch, her face still bent over to make sure it is executed properly, but her eyes raised toward the head of the bed. Her features are anxious, severe, even strained by her application to her work; or else by the anxiety afforded by this wounded man who has appeared so unexpectedly in her apartment; or else for some reason unknown to the latter.

"No," he says, "I don't need anything."

He speaks slowly, in a way that he himself finds surprising, the words abnormally distinct without his making them so intentionally.

"Are you in pain?"

"No," he says, "I can't . . . move . . . my body."

"You mustn't try to move. If you need something, ask me. It's because of the shot the doctor gave you. He'll try to come by tonight to give you another one." She has begun knitting again, her eyes lowered again over her work. "If he can," she says again. "No one can be sure of anything now."

It must also be the shot which gives the soldier this nausea he has been feeling since his awakening. He is thirsty; but he does not want to get up to drink from the faucet in the latrines down the hall. Instead he will wait until the attendant in the canvas duffle-coat and the hunter's boots comes back. No, that's not it: here, it is the woman with the low voice who is taking care of him. It is only at this moment that he is surprised to be back in this room whose setting belongs to a much earlier scene. He distinctly remembers the motorcycle, the dark hallway where he lay down in darkness against the door. Afterwards . . . He no longer knows what comes after: doubtless neither the hospital nor the busy café nor the long walk through the empty streets, now impossible in his condition. He asks:

"Is the wound serious?"

The woman continues knitting as if she had heard nothing.

He repeats: "What kind of wound is it?"

At the same time he realizes that he is not speaking loud enough, that his lips are forming the words, but without adding any force to them. The second time, however, the young woman has raised her head. She sets her work down on the table beside the large black ball of yarn and remains motionless, staring at him in silence, with a look of expectation, or anxiety, or fear. Finally she decides to ask: "Did you say something?"

He repeats his question again. This time weak but distinct sounds come out of his mouth, as if her voice with its extraordinary low intonations were restoring him the use of his own; unless the woman has guessed his words by reading them on his lips.

"No, it's nothing. It will all be over soon."

"To get up . . ."

"No, not today, and not tomorrow. A little later."

But he has no time to lose. He will get up tonight.

"The box," he says, "where is it?"

To make himself understood he must start over again: "The box . . . I had with me . . ."

A fleeting smile passes over the watchful face: "Don't worry, it's here. The boy brought it back. You mustn't talk so much. It's bad for you."

"No," the soldier says, "it isn't . . . very bad."

She has now picked up her knitting again; she continues to look at him, her hands resting on her knees. She resembles a statue. Her regular face with its sharp features recalls that of the woman who served him some wine one day, some other time, long ago. He makes an effort to say:

"I'm thirsty."

His lips have probably not even moved, for she neither stands up, nor answers, nor makes the slightest gesture. Moreover, her pale eyes had perhaps not even glanced at him, but at the other drinkers sitting farther away at other tables, toward the back of the room, where her gaze has now passed the soldier and his two companions, moving over the other tables along the wall where the small white bulletins are tacked whose fine-printed text still attracts a knot of readers, then the window with its pleated curtain at eye level and its three enameled balls on the outside of the glass and the snow behind it falling regularly and vertically in slow, heavy, close flakes.

And the new layer which gradually accumulates on the day's footprints, blurring angles, filling depressions, leveling surfaces, has quickly effaced the yellowish paths trampled by the pedestrians along the housefronts, the boy's isolated footprints, the two parallel furrows which the side car has made in the middle of the street.

But first he must make sure the snow is still falling. The soldier decides to ask the young woman about it. Does she even know, in this windowless room? She will have to look outside, to pass through the still open door back through the vestibule where the black umbrella is waiting, and through the long series of hallways, narrow staircases, and more hallways turning off at right angles, where she may easily get lost before reaching the street.

In any case it takes her a long time to come back, and it is now the boy who is sitting in her place at the table. He is wearing a turtle-neck sweater, short pants, wool socks, and felt slippers. He is sitting bolt upright without leaning against the back of the chair; his arms are stiff at his sides, his hands grasping the rattan arms of the chair; his bare legs sway between the front legs of the chair, making equal but opposite oscillations in two parallel planes. When he notices that the soldier is looking at him, he immediately stops moving; and, as if he had patiently waited for this moment to find out about something that is bothering him, he asks in his serious voice, which is not a child's voice at all:

"Why are you here?"

"I don't know," the soldier says.

The child has probably not heard the answer, for he repeats his question:

"Why didn't they put you in the barracks?"

The soldier no longer remembers whether or not he has asked the young woman about this matter. It is obviously not the boy who has brought him here, nor the lame man. He must also ask if someone has brought back the box wrapped in brown paper. The string no longer held, and the package must have come undone.

"Are you going to die here?" the child asks.

The soldier does not know the answer to this question either. Besides, he is amazed that it should even be asked. He tries to find explanations, but he has not even managed to formulate his anxiety when the boy has already turned away and is disappearing as fast as he can down the straight street, without even taking time to circle the cast-iron lampposts he passes, one after the other, without stopping. Soon only his footprints remain on the smooth surface of the fresh snow, their outline recognizable although deformed by his running, then becoming increasingly blurred as he runs faster and faster, finally growing quite vague, impossible to distinguish from the other footprints.

The young woman has not moved from her chair; and she answers quite readily, doubtless so that the wounded man will not worry. It is the child who has come to tell her that the soldier she had taken care of the day before was lying unconscious in a hallway a few streets away, curled up, no longer speaking, hearing nothing, moving no more than if he were dead. She had immediately decided to go to him. There was already a man standing beside the body, a civilian who happened to be passing at that moment, he said, but who in fact, seemed to have observed the entire scene from a distance, hidden in another doorway. She described him without any difficulty: a middle-aged man with thin gray hair, well dressed, with gloves, spats, and an ivory-handled umbrella. The umbrella was lying on the floor across the stoop, the door was wide open. The man was kneeling near the wounded man whose inert hand he was holding, grasping the wrist in order to take the pulse; he was a doctor, more or less, although not practicing. It is he who helped carry the body here.

As for the shoe box, the young woman had not noticed its precise location nor even its presence; it must have been nearby, shoved aside by the doctor in order to proceed more conveniently with his brief examination. Although his conclusions were hardly precise, he considered it was advisable in any case to put the wounded man to bed in a suitable place, despite the danger of moving him without a stretcher.

But they did not start out immediately, for no sooner had they decided to do so than the noise of the motorcycle had begun again. The man had quickly closed the door, and they had waited in the darkness until the danger was past. The motorcycle had come and gone several times, passing slowly through the neighboring streets, approaching, going away, approaching again, its maximum intensity soon diminishing at each passing, however, the machine exploring streets farther and farther away. When the noise was nothing more than a vague rumble, which they even had to strain to hear at all, the man opened the door again.

Everything was calm outside. From now on no one ventured out in the streets. A few scattered flakes of snow were falling through the motionless air. The two of them lifted the body, the man holding him by the thighs and the woman by the shoulders, under the arms. It was only then that she saw the blood which made a large stain on one side of the overcoat; but the doctor reassured her, declaring that it had nothing to do with the seriousness of the wound, and he carefully stepped off the stoop, skillfully carrying his share of the burden, followed by the young woman, who had more trouble keeping the soldier in a position she considered the least uncomfortable, struggling to maneuver this extremely heavy body, constantly changing her grip, and by doing so only succeeding in shaking him up more. Three steps ahead of them the boy was holding the umbrella in its black silk sheath in one hand and the shoe box in the other.

Then the doctor had to go home in order to get first aid supplies for the wounded man, until a hospital could take him (which might be some time, given the general disorganization). But when they had reached the young woman's apartment, which luckily was quite nearby, they again heard the sound of a motor, less distinct but more powerful. This time it was no longer merely a motorcycle but heavy cars or perhaps trucks. Therefore the man had to wait a while longer before daring to go outside again, and the three of them had remained in the room where they had laid the still unconscious soldier on the day bed. Standing motionless, they looked at him without speaking, the woman near the pillow leaning over his face, the man at the foot of the bed still wearing his gray leather gloves and his fur-lined coat, the child near the table with his cape and his beret on his head.

The soldier has also remained fully dressed: overcoat, leggings, and heavy boots. He is lying on his back, his eyes closed. He must be dead for the others to leave him like this. Yet the next scene shows him in the bed, the sheets pulled up to his chin, half listening to a confused story the same young woman with pale eyes is telling him: a slight difference of opinion having arisen between the kindly doctor with gray gloves and another individual whom she does not describe clearly but who must be the lame man. The latter must have returned to the house —much later, after the first injection—and wanted to do something which the other two, particularly the doctor, objected to. Although the basis of their disagreement is not easy to make out,

its violence is sufficiently indicated by the behavior of the antagonists, both of whom make a
number of expressive gesticulations, assume the-
atrical attitudes, and make exaggerated faces.
The lame man, leaning one hand on the table,
even finishes by brandishing his crutch at the
other; the doctor raises his arms to heaven, opening his hands like a prophet preaching a new
religion, or a dictator answering the cheers of
the crowd. The woman, frightened, steps to one
side to avoid the dispute; but without shifting
her other foot, she turns toward what she is
avoiding in order to follow the last exchanges
which threaten to become dramatic, while still
hiding her eyes behind her hands which are
spread before her face. The child is sitting on the
floor near an overturned chair; his legs are lying
flat forming a wide V; in his arms, against his
chest, he is holding the box wrapped in brown
paper.

Then come scenes still less distinct—still more
inaccurate, too, probably—violent although generally silent. They take place in vaguer, less char-
acterized, more impersonal areas; a staircase
recurs several times; someone is going down
it rapidly, holding onto the railing, taking several steps at the same time, almost flying from
one landing to the next, while the soldier, in
order not to be knocked over, is obliged to step

back into a corner. Then he goes more calmly down the stairs himself, and at the end of the long hallway he finds the snow-covered street again; and at the end of the street he finds the busy café again. Inside, everyone is as before: the bartender behind his bar, the doctor with the fur-lined coat in the group of middle-class citizens standing in front of the bar, but a little apart from the others and not participating in their conversation, the child sitting on the floor against a bench filled with drinkers near an overturned chair, still holding the box in his arms, and the young woman in the pleated dress with the dark hair and the graceful walk raising her tray with its single bottle over the heads of the seated drinkers, and finally the soldier sitting at the smallest table between his two comrades, who are ordinary infantrymen like himself, dressed as he is in overcoats buttoned to the neck and field caps, exhausted as he is, looking at nothing, as he is, sitting stiffly in their chairs and, like himself, saying nothing. All three have exactly the same face; the only difference among them is that one is seen from the left profile, the second full face, the third from the right profile; their six hands are resting on the table whose checkered oilcloth falls in rigid, conical folds at the corner of the table.

Does the waitress turn away from their mo-

tionless group now, presenting her classical profile toward the right, but with her body already
turned in the other direction, in the direction
of the man in middle-class clothes situated
slightly behind his own group, also seen in profile and from the same side, his features motionless like hers, like theirs? Someone else also
has an impassive face amid the agitation of the
entire company; it is the child sitting on the floor
in the foreground, on the parquet floor resembling that of the room itself, continuing the
latter, so to speak, after a brief separation which
consists of the horizontal strip of vertically-
striped wallpaper and then, lower down, the
three drawers of the chest.

The parquet floor extends beyond without
further interruption, to the heavy red curtains,
above which the fly's threadlike shadow continues its circuit across the white ceiling, now
passing close to the dark line that spoils the
uniformity of the surface near the angle of the
wall in the right corner, just within the field of
vision of the man lying on the day bed, the back
of his neck supported by the bolster.

He would have to get up in order to see at
close range just what this defect consists of: is
it actually a crack, or a spider web, or something else? He would probably have to stand on
a chair, or even on a ladder.

But once on his feet, other thoughts would quickly distract him from this project: the soldier would first of all have to find the shoe box again, probably put in another room now, in order to deliver it to its recipient. Since there can be no question of such a thing for the moment, the soldier need only remain motionless, lying on his back, his head raised slightly by the bolster, staring straight in front of him.

And yet his mind feels clearer, less drowsy, despite the persistent nausea and the progressive numbing of his entire body, which has grown worse since the second injection. It seems to him that the young woman who is leaning over him to give him something to drink is also looking at him more anxiously.

She speaks to him again about the lame man, against whom she seems to have some kind of grudge, or something even more violent. In her remarks she has already returned several times to this man who shares her apartment, apropos of other subjects, and always with a certain reticence, though at the same time revealing a need to explain her feelings on the matter, as if she were ashamed of this presence she was trying to justify, to destroy, and to minimize. Besides,

the young woman never explains the relation-
ship connecting them. She has had to struggle,
among other things, to keep the lame man from
opening the shoe box: he claimed it was essen-
tial to know what was in it. As a matter of fact,
she herself has wondered what should be done
with it . . .

"Nothing," the soldier says. "I'll take care of
it once I'm up."

"But," she says, "if it's something important
and you have to stay here for a while . . ." Suddenly she seems overcome with anxiety, and the
soldier supposes he himself is responsible for it
and would like to allay it.

"No," he says, "it's not so important."

"But what should be done with it?"

"I don't know."

"You were looking for someone. Was it to
give it to him?"

"Not necessarily. To him, or to someone else.
He would have told me who."

"Was it important for him?"

"It might be. I'm not sure."

"But what's in it?" She has spoken this last
sentence with such vehemence that he feels
obliged to tell her, as far as he is able, despite
the fatigue this conversation causes him, despite
his own lack of interest in this particular point,
despite his fear of disappointing her by the in-
significance of his answer:

"Not much, I think, I haven't looked, probably letters, papers, personal effects."

"It was for a friend?"

"No, someone I barely knew."

"Is he dead?"

"Yes, he died at the hospital. He was wounded in the stomach."

"And was it important for him?"

"Probably. He had asked for me and I came a few minutes too late. They gave me the box, from him. Then someone called him, on the telephone. I answered. I think it was his father or something. They didn't have the same name. I wanted to know what should be done with the box."

"And he asked you to meet him."

Yes; the man who telephoned has arranged to meet him in his own city, this one, where the soldier could try to go too, each henceforth doing whatever he could among this retreating army. The meeting place was not the man's house, for family reasons or something of that kind, but in the street, since all the cafés were closing, one after another. The soldier found a military truck carrying old uniforms which was going in this direction. Yet he had to come part of the way on foot.

He didn't know the city. He might have lost his way and gone to the wrong place. It was at a crossroads near a street light. He had not heard

clearly, or not remembered the names of the
streets. He has relied on topographical indica-
tions, following the prescribed itinerary as best
he could. When he thought he had reached the
place, he waited. The crossroads corresponded
to the description he had been given, but the
names of the streets did not sound like the
vaguely remembered consonants. He has waited
a long time, he has seen no one.

He was certain of the day, in any case. As
for the time, he had no watch. Perhaps he has
arrived too late. He has looked around the neighborhood. He has even waited at another crossroads identical to the first. He has wandered
through the whole city. He has returned several
times to the original place, insofar as he was
capable of recognizing it, that day and the days
following. In any case it was too late then.

"Only a few minutes. He had just died, before anyone had noticed. I had stayed in a café
with some non-coms, men I had never seen before. I didn't know. They told me to wait for a
friend of theirs, another man, a recruit. He was
at Reichenfels."

"Who was at Reichenfels?" the woman asks.
She leans a little closer to the bed. Her low voice
fills the whole room as she insists: "Who? In
which regiment?"

"I don't know. Someone. The doctor was

there too, with his gray ring, leaning on the counter, and the wife, the lame man's wife, the one who poured the wine."

"What are you talking about?"

Her face is quite close to his. Her pale, dark-rimmed eyes are made even larger by the widening of the lids.

"I have to go get the box," he says. "It must be back at the barracks. I forgot it. It's on the bed, behind the bolster . . ."

"Lie still, rest. Don't try to talk any more."

She holds out her hand to pull up the sheet. The palm and the inner surface of the fingers show black stains, as though from paint or grease, which have resisted washing.

"Who are you?" the soldier says. "What should I call you? What's your name? . . ."

But she no longer seems to hear him. She arranges the sheets and the pillow, straightens the blanket.

"Your hand," the soldier says again. This time he cannot proceed further.

"Lie still," she says, "it's nothing. It's from carrying you. The overcoat had fresh stains on the sleeve."

They stumble at every step over the ruts and soft earth, the darkness illuminated only occasionally by fleeting gleams. Both men have abandoned their knapsacks. The wounded man has also left his rifle behind. But the soldier has kept his, even though its strap has just broken and he is obliged to carry it in his hand, horizontally. Three steps ahead, the boy is carrying the umbrella in the same way. The wounded man grows heavier and heavier and clings to the soldier's neck, making it still more difficult for the latter to walk. Now he can no longer move at all: neither his arms nor even his head. He can only look straight ahead at the leg of the table from which the oilcloth has been removed, the table leg now visible all the way to the top: it ends in a sphere supporting a cube, or rather an almost cubical parallelepiped, with square horizontal surfaces but rectangular vertical ones; the vertical surface has a design carved within a rectangular frame following the shape of the surface itself: a kind of stylized floret, its straight stem splitting near the top into two small symmetrical arcs on either side, like a V with curved branches, the concavity toward the bottom, slightly shorter than the terminal portion of the axial stem starting from the same point, and . . . , his eyes no longer able to remain lowered so long, his gaze is obliged to move up the length of the red curtains to the ceiling and the hair-thin, somewhat sinuous crack whose shape also has something distinct and complicated about it which it would be necessary to follow with application from one turn to the next, with its curves, vacillations, uncertainties, sudden changes of directions, inflections, continuations, slight regressions, but it would take more time, a little time, a few minutes, a few seconds, and it is already, now, too late.

On my last visit, the third injection was useless. The wounded soldier was dead. The streets are full of armed soldiers who march by singing in low voices, their songs more nostalgic than joyous. Others pass in open trucks in which the men are sitting stiffly, rifles upright, held in both hands between their knees; they are arranged in two rows, back to back, each row facing one side of the street. Patrols circulate everywhere, and no one may go out after nightfall without a pass. Yet I had to give the third injection, and only a practicing doctor would have had authorization to do so. Fortunately the streets were poorly lit, certainly much worse than during the last few days when the lights were on even in broad daylight. But it was too late for the injection. Besides, they only served to make the dying man's last hours less painful. There was nothing else to do.

The body has remained in the apartment of

the sham lame man, who will make the proper declaration, telling the whole story as it actually happened: a wounded man whom they took in off the street and about whom they knew nothing, not even his name, since he had no papers. If the man is afraid his leg will be examined on this occasion and his actual condition discovered, the woman could take the appropriate steps; as for the man, he need only avoid showing himself when they come to get the body: it will not be the first time he has hidden from a visitor.

The woman seems to mistrust him. In any case she has been unwilling to let him deal with the package wrapped in brown paper which he badly wanted to open. He thought it was some secret weapon, or at least its plans. The box is now in safe keeping—on the cracked black marble top of the chest—closed, wrapped up again, retied, but bringing it back here from their place has not been easy on account of the patrols. Luckily it was not very far. Just before the goal was reached, a brief command rang out: "Halt!" shouted in a loud voice from some distance behind. In itself, the box was obviously not very compromising; the sham lame man's notions on this subject were, of course, ridiculous, but the woman was nevertheless afraid that the letters the soldier had mentioned to her might contain information of a non-personal nature, of military

or political interest, for instance, the soldier himself having shown in many circumstances an exaggerated discretion in their regard. It would
be better, in any case, not to let them be taken,
particularly since the dagger-bayonet the woman
also returned at the same time might seem quite
suspicious. The lack of a pass would have made
the bearer's case still worse. The loud, command-
ing voice has shouted "Halt!" a second time, then
a third, and immediately afterward there was a
rapid burst of machine-gun fire. But the gun must
have been too far away to aim properly, and it
was very dark in this area. Perhaps it was even
fired into the air. Once past the street corner,
there was no longer any danger. The apartment
house door had not remained ajar, of course.
Nevertheless the key has turned noiselessly in
the lock, the hinges have not creaked, the door
has closed in silence.

At first glance the letters contain no secret of
any kind and are of no general or personal importance. They are ordinary letters, the kind a
country girl sends every week to her fiancé, giving news of the farm or the neighbors, regularly
repeating the same conventional formulas about
separation and return. The box also contains an
old gold watch, of no particular value, with a
tarnished gilded-brass chain; there is no name
engraved inside the lid over the watch face; there

is also a ring, a signet ring made of silver or nickel alloy, the kind workers often make for themselves in factories, with "H. M." engraved on it; finally, a dagger-bayonet of the current model, identical in every detail to the one given by the young woman, along with the package whose origin she was unwilling to specify, saying only that she was afraid to keep it at home since the latest regulations concerning the surrender of weapons, but that even so she did not want to turn it in (it is certainly the sham lame man who has forced her to get rid of it). The box is not a shoe box, it is a biscuit box of the same dimensions, but made out of tin.

What is most important about all this is the envelopes of the letters: they are addressed to a soldier—Henri Martin—and give his postal sector. On the back is the name and address of the girl who has written them. It is to her that the box will have to be sent when the mails are functioning again, since it is now impossible to find the father, who is not even named Martin. Besides, he had probably proposed himself as the provisional recipient only for reasons of convenience: even if he knew the contents of the box, he supposed it would be easier, geographically speaking, to reach him than the girl herself. Unless only the letters are intended for the latter, the dagger, the watch, and the ring belonging by rights to the father. It might also be supposed that the letters too should not be returned to their sender; many reasons might readily be suggested in support of this notion.

Rather than send the package through the mails, it would probably be preferable to carry it in one's own hands and return it with the customary considerations. As a matter of fact the girl might not yet have been informed of her fiancé's death. Only the father was notified when he telephoned the hospital; yet supposing that he is not the real father—or not legally the father, or in any case not quite the father—he is not obliged to be in communication with the girl, or even to know of her existence; so there is no reason for him to write her once the mails are functioning again.

The woman who has taken care of the wounded soldier has obtained no information from him as to his comrade who died before he did. Toward the end he talked a good deal, but he had already forgotten most things that had happened recently; besides, he was delirious most of the time. The woman declares that he was already sick before he was wounded, that he had fever, and that he sometimes behaved like a sleepwalker. Her son, a serious-looking boy of about ten, had already encountered him in the street, perhaps even several times, if it is

actually the same boy each time, as is likely
despite slight contradictions. His role is signifi-
cant since he is the one who, by his heedlessness,
has provoked the actions of the occupants of the
side car, but his many appearances are not all
decisive to the same degree. The lame man, on
the other hand, plays virtually no part at all. His
presence in the morning at the Rue Bouvet military offices (transformed into a barracks or hospitalization center) has nothing surprising about
it, given the ease with which he maneuvers when
no one is there to observe his means of locomo-
tion. Besides, the soldier does not seem to have
paid much attention to his remarks. The bartender, for his part, is problematical or insignificant. He does not say a word, does not make a
move; this heavy-set bald man might also be a
spy or an informer, the nature of his reflections
is impossible to determine. The minor characters
arguing in front of him with so much animation
will, in any case, tell him nothing worth reporting
to his eventual chiefs; they are only café strate-
gists who make History over as they please,
criticizing the ministers, correcting the generals,
creating imaginary incidents which among other
things might have permitted a victory at Reichenfels. The soldier sitting in the back of the room
at the next to the last table to the right certainly
has a more realistic outlook on battles; hence he

has nothing to say about them; he must merely be waiting to be served something to drink, between his two comrades whose faces are not entirely visible, the one seen in profile and the other three-quarters from the rear. His first change of uniform can be explained by the general and probably unjustified contempt to which his regiment has been subjected since the defeat; he has preferred wearing less familiar insignia on this trip.

Hence he can mingle with the crowd without attracting attention, and quietly drink the wine the waitress is about to serve him. Meanwhile he stares straight ahead through the large window. The snow has stopped falling. The weather has grown increasingly mild during the course of the day. The sidewalks are still white, but the street, where the trucks have been passing continuously for hours, has already turned black again along its entire central section, the half melted snow having been heaped in the gutters on either side; each time the soldier crosses a side street, he sinks in up to his leggings with a spongy noise, while the scattered drops of fine rain begin to float in the evening air, still mixed with a few moist snowflakes which turn to water even before they have reached the street.

The soldier hesitates to leave the busy café where he has come in to rest for a moment. It is the rain he is staring at through the large window with its pleated curtains and its three billiard balls on the other side of the glass. The child is also watching the rain, sitting on the floor close to the window so that he can see through the thin material. It begins to rain much harder. The umbrella in its black silk sheath is leaning on the coat rack near the fur-lined overcoat. But in the drawing there are so many other garments hanging on top of each other that it is difficult to make out much of anything in the jumble. Just under the picture is the chest with its three drawers whose gleaming front is fitted with two large, tarnished brass knobs. In the bottom drawer is the biscuit box wrapped in brown paper. The rest of the room is unchanged: the ashes in the fireplace, the sheets of paper scattered on top of the table, the burnt cigarette butts filling the ashtray, the table lamp turned on, the heavy red curtains drawn tight.

Outside it is raining. Outside you walk through the rain with your head down, shielding your eyes with one hand while you stare ahead, a few yards ahead, at a few yards of wet asphalt. The rain does not get in here, nor the snow nor the wind; and the only dust that dulls the gleaming horizontal surfaces, the polished wood of the table, the waxed parquet floor, the marble mantlepiece, the cracked marble top of the chest,

the only dust comes from the room itself, perhaps from the cracks in the floor, or else from
the bed, or from the ashes in the fireplace, or
from the velvet curtains whose vertical folds rise
from the floor to the ceiling across which the
fly's shadow—which is shaped like the incandescent thread of the electric bulb concealed by the
truncated conical lampshade—now passes near
the tiny black line which, remaining in the half-
darkness beyond the circle of light and at a
distance of four or five yards, is extremely difficult to make out: first a short, straight segment
about half an inch long, followed by a series of
rapid undulations, themselves scalloped . . .
But the image grows blurred by trying to distinguish the outlines, as in the case of the in-
ordinately delicate pattern of the wallpaper and
the indeterminate edges of the gleaming paths
made in the dust by the felt slippers, and, beyond
the door, the dark vestibule where the umbrella
is leaning against the coat rack, then, once past
the entrance door, the series of long hallways,
the spiral staircase, the door to the building with
its stone stoop, and the whole city behind me.